"MAYBE YOU'D COME
A LITTLE CLOSER . . ."

He was reaching over to pull her across his lap as he spoke.

"We have to plan the rest of our cruise."

By then, Stephanie's heart had abandoned its regular cadence and was thumping violently. She was sure Cole could feel it as his hand fumbled momentarily with the buttons of her pajama top before moving gently but possessively over her, leaving her skin on fire with longing. And then his mouth came down, eventually finding her lips in a kiss that made time stand still.

When he finally raised his head, he shook it slightly and gave her glowing face a wry look. "If you knew how long I've been wanting to do that . . ."

ISLAND RENDEZVOUS

Island
Rendezvous

by

Glenna Finley

"My rendezvous is appointed, it is certain,
—and the lover true for whom I pine will be there."
—WALT WHITMAN

A SIGNET BOOK

SIGNET
Published by the Penguin Group
Penguin Books USA Inc., 375 Hudson Street,
New York, New York 10014, U.S.A.
Penguin Books Ltd, 27 Wrights Lane,
London W8 5TZ, England
Penguin Books Australia Ltd, Ringwood,
Victoria, Australia
Penguin Books Canada Ltd, 2801 John Street,
Markham, Ontario, Canada L3R 1B4
Penguin Books (N.Z.) Ltd, 182–190 Wairau Road,
Auckland 10, New Zealand

Penguin Books Ltd, Registered Offices:
Harmondsworth, Middlesex, England

First published by Signet, an imprint of New American Library,
a division of Penguin Books USA Inc.

First Printing, September, 1990
10 9 8 7 6 5 4 3 2 1

REGISTERED TRADEMARK—MARCA REGISTRADA

Printed in the United States of America

*For
Duncan, Eleanor, and Elizabeth,
my favorite crew!*

Chapter 1

"Would you please say that again?" Stephanie asked the resort manager, trying to keep the disbelief from her voice.

"I said, Miss Church, that you've missed the boat. Or rather that there simply is no boat for you." William Stacy, the resort manager, sounded harassed as he flipped through the papers atop his desk. "We did notify your office as soon as we knew about this development two days ago."

"I left New York three days ago," Stephanie pointed out.

"We discovered that. Naturally we will compliment your stay here at Harbour Cay for a few extra days until you can change your travel plans. Unfortunately that's all we can do."

The man fiddled absently with a pencil as he watched her reaction to his pronouncement. The disappointment on her face wasn't surprising, but it was a pity, he decided. Quite different from her appearance when she had first entered his office. It had been hard to mask his admiration then because blue-eyed natural blondes were worth a second look anywhere. On Tortola in the British Virgin Islands they were almost as rare as snow in July, especially when they came as attractively packaged as the woman in front of him.

The manager shook his head sadly, wishing he could bring a smile back to the young woman's features and still convince her to follow his advice.

"Are you sure there won't be another schedule change?" Stephanie was asking. "Maybe you could shift a few reservations so I could still have a firsthand experience with bare-boating down here. My firm would really appreciate it."

"Naturally we always try to cooperate with travel firms," Stacy said, his tone stiffening. "However, when I called your office to announce the change of plans, your employer was very cooperative. He understood that we can't turn down valid customers, especially at this time of year." He paused as he glimpsed someone in the open office doorway behind her and bounced to his feet. "Ah, yes—Mr. Warner. How did you find the *Bagatelle*? Everything satisfactory?"

"It looks okay."

Stephanie turned around, annoyed to find a tall, dark-haired man lounging against the door frame. He was wearing faded blue denims and a worn T-shirt that must have shrunk on repeated washings because it didn't have a spare inch of material, faithfully revealing impressive shoulders and a lean waistline. Show-off, she thought disdainfully as her glance wandered over him.

Evidently her feelings must have been more revealing than she knew because the man's eyebrows rose slowly as he surveyed her in turn, and the expression on his tanned face hardened perceptibly. "I'm sorry," he bit out the words tersely, "I didn't mean to interrupt. Maybe when you're not busy, Stacy . . ." He let his voice trail off.

"You're not interrupting," the hotel manager insisted.

"I'll be in the bar," the man finished. With a nod that included both of them, he turned on his heel and disappeared.

"Yes, well, was there anything else, Miss Church?" The manager started edging around his desk, obviously intent on bringing her interview to a close so he could pursue the man who'd just left.

Stephanie felt her last hopes of a boating vacation slipping away. "Maybe you could just check your records again and see if somebody needs a crew," she asked, hating the desperate note in her voice.

He shot her a suspicious look. "I thought you said that you had very little sailing experience."

A flush rose under her cheekbones. "Well, how about a cook? I *do* know how to do that."

"We have employees to fill these positions." He started for the door, ushering her ahead of him. "Unless there's something else you can do, I'm afraid you're out of luck."

His innuendo wasn't lost on Stephanie; her back stiffened. "That's as far as my talents go," she snapped, letting him know she didn't appreciate his remark.

He shrugged, obviously finished with the discussion. "In that case, you'll just have to enjoy the island while you're here. I can recommend the ferry over to St. Thomas if you get bored on Tortola. I'll have to warn you, though, that we're fully booked for the weekend, so you'll need to find other accommodation by then. I am sorry about this, Miss Church."

He gave her another smile that didn't reach his eyes, and closed his office door behind her as soon as she crossed the threshold.

Stephanie muttered a disgusted "I'll bet" before slowly heading toward the swimming-pool area and the path toward her room.

She scuffed at the tiled floor as she walked along, lingering in the outdoor bar area long enough to survey the long docks where the charter boats were moored. The place was a hive of activity, with sleek schooners being readied by a throng of Harbour Cay employees. Some were carrying provisions down the wooden piers for the outgoing boats while others were industriously cleaning the new arrivals at the end of their charters. Sandwiched in between the natives on the piers were groups of sunburned boaters, obviously delighted with their holidays as they recounted their adventures.

Stephanie's lips thinned as she surveyed them, knowing that her own vacation plans had been effectively quashed. The prospect of a few days sightseeing—even in the British Virgins—paled when compared with her previous plans for a week of soaking up the sunshine on a thirty-seven-foot schooner.

"Damn," she muttered as she watched the carefree vacationers on the piers. "Damn! Damn! Damn!"

"Are you mad at anyone in particular or just the world in general?"

Stephanie whirled at the sound of the masculine voice next to her ear and found herself staring at the man who'd given her the cool appraisal from the manager's doorway a few minutes earlier. He didn't look much more forthcoming now, she thought as she struggled for a coherent reply.

"You weren't at a loss for words a little while ago," he went on dispassionately. "Or do you need a formal introduction before you talk to strangers?"

Stephanie's lips tightened even more, seeing the sardonic glint in his eyes. "It depends," she replied.

"On what?"

"On whom," she corrected, glad that he couldn't know how hard her heart was pounding just then.

"I wondered if you still wanted to take a boat ride. The one that Stacy"—he jerked a thumb toward the manager's office—"told you was out of the question."

Stephanie had to swallow before she could get her answer out. "Exactly what did you have in mind?"

A faint glimmer of amusement lightened his features as he said, "Not what *you* have in mind, if your expression is any indication. Evidently you haven't spent much time in a thirty-seven-foot sloop if you're hoping for unbridled lust and passion. You're more apt to end up seasick and soaking wet in these waters."

Color rose under her cheekbones at the ease with which he'd read her thoughts. "I just wondered if you wanted a crew or a cook?" she told him, crossing her fingers behind her cotton skirt. "Or maybe you already have them," she added hopefully.

He shook his head. "Thirty-seven feet, remember?" Then, nodding toward the line of boats tied up at the pier in front of them, he added, "You're getting it confused with a fifty-one-footer. Then you can talk about crew and cook."

By that time, Stephanie was so confused that she would have had trouble separating a Boston

Whaler from a power cruiser, but she wasn't about to admit it. "Mr. Stacy's cancellation wasn't the end of the world," she said defiantly, knowing that her chances were going a-glimmering with every word but determined to keep her pride intact. "I'm sure that I'll survive."

"There's no doubt about that," he said, cutting into her protests ruthlessly. "If you'll belt up long enough to let me get a word in, I was about to explain."

"Well, naturally—"

"I do need a crew of sorts," he went on carelessly, "so you'd have to take your turn at the wheel during the day, and help with setting the anchor at night. As far as the cooking goes, I'd planned to eat ashore most of the time. Naturally, I'd cover your expenses, since you'd be doing me a favor by coming along."

"Setting the anchor," she murmured, still occupied with the jobs he'd mentioned.

"That's right." He shot a frowning glance down at her troubled face. "You do know a little bit about sailing, don't you? You must," he went on then without waiting for her confirmation. "Otherwise you wouldn't be here. If you wanted a comfortable life on the water, you'd be aboard that steady stream of cruise boats going in and out of St. Thomas."

His tone made it evident what he thought of quick Caribbean cruises, and all Stephanie had to do was shrug and say, "There's not much fun in that."

"My feelings exactly." He shoved his hands in the pockets of his denims and surveyed her approvingly. "Have we got a deal, then?"

"You bet," Stephanie agreed without hesitation. She was hoping she could be safely aboard before he had second thoughts about her sailing credentials. "You haven't said how long you planned for this island-hopping expedition. I only have a week's vacation."

"That should do. The distances are short down here, and if I decide to add a few days at the end, I can bring you back here in time to make your plane reservation back to the States."

"That sounds fine." On the point of asking when he wanted her aboard, a sudden thought struck. "Good Lord, I don't even know your name—or anything about you."

"Cole Warner." He extended his hand in a businesslike manner. "What's yours?"

"Stephanie. Stephanie Church." And then shook hands with him solemnly as she added, "From New York. A reluctant transplant from the Midwest."

"A lot of New Yorkers are," he commented. "I'm a transplant myself. Does that make all this respectable enough now, or do I have to call in some character witnesses?"

Her eyebrows went up. "Do you have any here?"

"Not really," he confessed. "Otherwise I wouldn't be recruiting you, would I?" He saw her start to frown and went on hurriedly, "I've a small acquaintance with the manager in there. But all he could tell you is that I pay my bills. I took out a boat here about a month ago."

Stephanie started to ask, "By yourself?" but closed her lips again, strangely reluctant to pry into his personal life. Finally she took a deep breath and asked, "Is there a Mrs. Warner at home?"

His slow grin made him look younger than the mid-thirties she'd estimated earlier. "Only my mother. And no serious commitments either. How about you?" he asked casually, showing it hadn't occurred to him before.

"Free, white, and more than twenty-one," she assured him.

He surveyed her through half-closed eyes. "Not by much, I'd guess."

"I'm twenty-five. Not that it matters. Are there any other questions?"

"Only if you can be ready to sail today. You'll need to come aboard for the checkout cruise this afternoon."

Her face paled at his last announcement. "What do you mean—checkout cruise?"

"You make it sound like a polygraph test," he said with amusement. "It's a requirement of the management here. They want to make sure we don't sink half their fleet getting away from the dock or lose the mainsail if the wind shifts. A thirty-seven-foot sloop is a considerable investment these days, and they can't afford any ham-handed skippers. I had to complete a résumé of my experience before I took out a boat the first time down here."

"They'll need a résumé of *my* sailing experience?" Her voice rose, taut with nerves.

"You misunderstood me. They only care about *my* experience. Sailing experience," he added, seeing her frown. "All you have to do is follow my orders. You can manage that, can't you?"

Hearing the sudden doubts in his tone, Stephanie switched tactics quickly. It was going to be hard enough to pass whatever the checkout involved without putting extra doubts in Cole Warner's mind at this stage—especially since his was the only offer forthcoming and it certainly was better than an occasional ferry ride over to St. Thomas for her "saltwater experience."

"I'm not a complete novice," she assured him, trying to sound as if she meant it. "I crewed for a friend of mine who races—although that was a little while ago," she added, feeling she'd better stick to honesty. "I suspect it's like riding a bicycle: everything will come back once we get away from the dock. And speaking of that, when do I go aboard?"

She felt a moment's disquiet as she saw a frown go over his face. Obviously she hadn't been as convincing as she'd hoped. Finally, he shrugged and said, "Two o'clock. The *Bagatelle*'s down at Slip Forty-two. Get one of the bellmen to carry your stuff down."

"The *Bagatelle*?"

"That's the name of the boat." There was no hiding his impatient undertones then.

Stephanie swallowed, realizing that if she continued with her inane questions the man was definitely going to have second thoughts. From the way his jaw had clenched, she might have gone too far already. "Right," she said briskly. "The *Bagatelle* at two o'clock. I'll be there—don't worry." With a nod, she quickly skirted around the tiled swimming pool and headed toward her room. Once she'd reached the far wing of the resort and climbed the stairs to the upper level, she risked a look behind her and gave a sigh of relief that Cole Warner hadn't followed her to say he'd changed his mind.

The tastefully decorated interior of her room normally would have tempted her to kick off her shoes and head to the balcony that overlooked the long docks of the marina. Instead, she went over and closed the balcony's louvered doors. The telephone beside the bed got her attention next and she took the receiver off the stand and placed it carefully on the table. If Cole Warner was having a change of heart, she wasn't going to make it easy for him.

Almost absently she reached for the switch to start the big ceiling fan in the center of the room. The immediate circulation of air made her nod approvingly, but even then, she detoured by the adjoining bathroom to rinse her face with cool water. Midday humidity in the

British Virgin Islands during late May wasn't something that the Chamber of Commerce publicized, but it had taken only a night's stay for Stephanie to realize that anything more than shorts and a halter felt like a shroud when the sun came out. Another definite advantage to being on a boat, she told herself as she patted her face dry and then surveyed her reflection in the mirror above the basin. She peered more closely, wondering if the freckles on her nose had some recruits—certainly the sun had brought a distinctly pinkish tinge to her forehead. If she didn't use some sunscreen on the boat, she was going to look grilled before they got fifty feet from the dock. For an instant, she thought about Cole Warner's smooth tan. With that dark hair, he could stroll through the park and end up looking as if he'd spent a weekend at Palm Springs.

Stephanie wrinkled her nose derisively as she looked in the mirror again. Her fair hair was escaping from the chignon style she'd chosen earlier for its practicality in the hot weather. Unless she worked at preservation, every bit of curl in her hair would disappear in the first whiff of a salt breeze, and her skin would look like an underdone lamb chop.

Which is what happens when people go sailing, she told herself as she put the towel back on the rack and headed back into the bedroom. Instead of checking on her appearance, she'd be better off to detour by the gift shop and see if she could pick up a cookbook with some "Meals Afloat" recipes, in case her employer changed his mind about eating ashore. Even a scant acquaintance with Cole Warner made her suspect that he wasn't going to be impressed with her measurements when he was hoping for a nicely broiled porterhouse.

Her heart sank as she mentally reviewed the way he'd looked as they parted. Probably the only way she'd get off the dock would be if she kept very quiet and behaved as if she were practicing for the America's Cup until they were safely away from Tortola.

A sudden beeping noise drew her over to the telephone. She hesitated for a moment and then replaced the receiver on the hook. Almost immediately it rang. She lifted the handset and put it to her ear, dreading to hear the voice at the other end. When it turned out to be feminine with a British accent, she was so relieved that she sank down on the edge of the bed.

"Miss Church, this is the hotel operator. Was your telephone receiver off the hook?"

Stephanie had to clear her throat before she could reply. "I'm not sure. At any rate, it seems to be working fine now. Could you transfer me to a bellman, please? I'd like to have my luggage picked up in a little while."

"Of course. Stay on the line."

There was a considerable delay before someone answered the phone again, but a male voice finally assured her that her cases would be picked up at one-forty-five as she requested and transferred to Slip Forty-two.

"And I absolutely can't be late," she told him before he could hang up.

"We do it all the time, miss," was his calm reply, indicating that she could have a nervous breakdown about it but that he wasn't planning to.

"All right. Thank you," she said meekly, and hung up. She'd done all she could do for the present. If there was a slipup later, she'd drag her bags down the dock herself to make sure she was on the *Bagatelle* when it sailed. As she wandered over to glance through the louvered doors out onto the balcony and the docks beyond, she tried to remember what a bagatelle was, and decided she'd have to ask Cole if she couldn't find a dictionary in the interval.

She looked at her watch and tried to decide how to fill the two and a half hours until she was due to board the boat. Packing came first, of course, but that would take only fifteen minutes at the most. Then there was the matter of lunch and, later, checking out. She'd have to eat, she thought as she went to the closet and pulled out her suitcase, opening it on the bed. Normally she'd have gone down to the coffee shop by the pool and ordered something, but there was also a good chance that Cole Warner planned to do exactly the same thing. And until she was aboard the *Bagatelle* and they were out in midchannel, she didn't want to risk any unnecessary encounters with the man.

That left room service or a quick trip to Road Town, she decided as she took two dresses and a raincoat from the closet and automatically folded the former into her bag.

By the time she'd finished her packing a few minutes later, she'd decided in favor of a quick cab ride into Road Town, which was about ten minutes down the winding two-lane road. That way, she was less apt to see anyone she knew. The main thing was to make sure that she was back in plenty of time to check out and get down to the dock.

When she had accomplished all her tasks and put her cases by the door so that there wouldn't be any delay when she returned, she'd changed into a pair of white slacks and a striped cotton shirt. She dropped a small-brimmed cotton hat atop the cases so she'd have it handy.

Fortunately there was a cab waiting at the stand by the office. Stephanie gingerly tapped the sleeping driver on the shoulder and waited for him to push a hat up from his face before she asked if he could make the trip into Road Town, the main village on the island.

"Yes, ma'am, I s'pose so." He sounded reluctant to abandon his midday siesta, but he managed to get out and open the rear door of the car for her.

Stephanie thanked him and waited until he'd gotten behind the steering wheel again before asking, "Would it be possible for you to wait for me while I have lunch downtown?" And then, when she saw him start to frown, she added hastily, "I'll pay for your waiting time, of course."

"How 'bout I come back and pick you up at a certain time?" he countered after thinking it over.

"I guess that would be all right," she said reluctantly. "If you'll be sure to be there."

"No problem, lady." He started the car and made an illegal U-turn in the cramped space of the entranceway, narrowly missing a cart full of supplies that was being wheeled toward the marina entrance. He ignored the shouted epithets as he accelerated and Stephanie sank back on the cracked vinyl seat.

She breathed a sigh of relief when they emerged on the two-lane pavement into Road Town, feeling somehow that she'd escaped again. Which was absurd, she told herself. There was no reason to worry about crewing on a sloop with a perfect stranger. Half the inhabitants on the island of Tortola seemed to be either getting on a boat or just coming off one, and it would be nice to join the party.

The island natives probably thought such activity was typical tourist fare, Stephanie decided as her driver pulled up on the narrow shoulder of the road to invite a woman and her small child into the front seat, saving them a walk in the hot sun.

The woman was dressed in a bright-yellow skirt and a sleeveless blouse of red cotton while the youngster wore brief boxer shorts. He glanced over the back of the seat to stare solemnly at Stephanie once the driver pulled onto the road again, and broke into giggles when she winked at him. That brought his mother's head around and she smiled too, murmuring a soft " 'Afternoon, miss" before facing the front again.

By then, the thick row of palm trees bordering the side of the road had been replaced by small shops and one mini-size supermarket with a crowded parking lot. Apparently the inhabitants of Tortola watched the grocery prices as carefully as shoppers in the States, Stephanie concluded.

There was a decided difference in the outer characteristics of the residents, though. Most people were dressed in the minimum amount of clothing that decency allowed. It wasn't surprising, considering the midday temperature. The hot air coming through the open windows of the old taxi had a tropical tang with overtones of baked earth, saltwater, and thick tropical vegetation. If they could bottle it, it was worth a fortune, Stephanie thought, taking a deep satisfied breath as she realized how lucky she was to be there.

By then, the scattered shops had become a solid line as they drove into the center of Road Town, although all the commerce was only one block deep facing the water. The driver pulled up in front of one of the biggest establishments—a combination gift shop and coffee bar opposite the ferry landing—and got out of the car to help Stephanie alight.

They held an earnest conversation then about the time he was to return and pick her up. It concluded with the driver promising solemnly that he would be there unless an act of God intervened.

She watched him drive off. He was already in hilarious conversation with his friends on the front seat of the cab and she wondered just how binding their agreement would turn out to be.

She shrugged, deciding that there was no use worrying and ruining her lunch in the bargain. Especially since she was going to have really important things to worry about later in the afternoon when she faced Cole Warner and boarded the *Bagatelle*.

The coffee bar was furnished in the style of a ship's cabin with driftwood gray paneling and anchors deposited in any empty spaces. Fortunately the cook turned out a most acceptable club sandwich and cup of coffee in record time. Even so, a glance at her watch convinced Stephanie to skip dessert and be early on the curb for her assigned taxi.

She gave a reluctant glance toward the gift shop after paying her lunch check and then remembered that she'd be back in town after the cruise. She'd just have to make sure that she had time for purchasing a few momentos for the people in the office before she got on the small plane back to Puerto Rico and then home.

As she walked down the gravel path toward the street, she wondered whether Cole would allow time for shopping forays if they stopped at Virgin Gorda or Peter Island. Probably not, she decided, remembering that most men would rather read a week-old newspaper than drag around a gift or souvenir shop. Probably it was just as well, she concluded, since her luggage was already stuffed to capacity and her wallet wasn't.

She didn't have to wait long for the traffic to pass when she reached the main street. There was one local bus with four or five passengers relaxing inside. It was easy to check on their mood because the bus sides were solid only to window level and from there on up, it was open to the breezes aside from a few supports for the top.

When Stephanie reached the other side of the street, she looked around anxiously for her taxi-cab and then relaxed a bit when she realized that she was ten minutes early for the appointed time.

While she waited on the wide parking strip next to the harbor wall, she stared with interest at a flotilla of work boats tied up nearby. There weren't many pleasure craft aside from a few small sailboats bobbing from their mooring buoys out in the harbor. Evidently most of the visitors concentrated on the bigger marinas on the outer edges of town.

She looked around for a patch of shade after checking her watch again, aware that the hot humid air was suddenly overpowering. Mopping her damp cheeks with the back of her hand didn't help much, and she found herself wishing that she'd had a frosty glass of iced tea for lunch instead of the bitter cup of coffee that was served from a warming plate.

She cast another hopeful glance down the street and then smiled as she saw her taxi approaching. She opened the rear door when he pulled alongside, and hurriedly slid onto the seat so that they wouldn't hold up traffic.

"Thank you for being so prompt," she said, reaching in her purse to pull out a handerchief and blot her forehead as he started off again.

"That's okay. You sounded as if you'd be early, and you don't want to be standing out in this midday sun too long."

The familiar "mad dogs and Englishmen" label evidently applied to American tourists as far as the natives were concerned, she decided. "If I'd stood there much longer, I'd just have been a spot on the pavement. At least, that's the way it felt."

He nodded, meeting her glance in the rear-vision mirror. "Folks have to learn to slow down when they get to the islands. You're lucky on the weather, though. Last week it rained every day."

That comment seemed to exhaust his interest in the weather and for the rest of the trip he was content to wave and shout greetings to acquaintances walking on the roadside as if they had all the time in the world to get home. Finally, as he turned the cab into the marina entrance, he slowed and gestured toward a small building on the left. "You want to stock up on supplies, or have you already taken care of that?"

"I—I think it's already taken care of," she told him. "I'm just crewing on this trip," she added, hoping that she sounded as if cruising was a major part of her life.

After they arrived at the cul-de-sac by the office and she'd paid the fare, the man unbent enough to smile and say, "Have a good trip. It looks like fair weather, so you won't have to worry about that."

Stephanie chuckled as she walked toward the path leading to her room. Of all the things she'd been worrying about, fair weather hadn't even been on the list. Once back in her room, she cast a longing glance toward her suitcase where she'd packed her shorts and then shook her head. Even though they'd be cooler, she was afraid the sunscreen might not work and she simply couldn't take the chance of getting burned on the first day out. Besides, there'd be a breeze on the water, she told herself.

When the bellman came a few minutes later, she asked him to take her luggage to Slip Forty-two while she checked out at the cashier's desk. His casual nod showed that it was a familiar order, and Stephanie waited for him to disappear down the walkway before muttering a "Hallelujah" under her breath. Everything was going so smoothly, she felt like pinching herself to be sure she was awake.

Even the cashier seemed exceptionally pleasant when she paid her bill. It wasn't until the manager wandered by as Stephanie was replacing her credit card in her wallet that the first discordant note was sounded. " 'Afternoon, Miss Church," he said briskly, and then seeing the receipt the cashier had pushed toward her, he frowned and added, "What's this? You're not leaving? I specified that you could have your room until the end of the week. There's no cause for hard feelings. After all, we've dealt with your firm for some years now."

"There are no hard feelings, Mr. Stacy. My plans have changed, that's all." She couldn't keep a triumphant note from her voice as she announced, "I've been invited to crew on the *Bagatelle* and we're leaving shortly."

The man's thin features looked distinctly disapproving suddenly. "The *Bagatelle*, you say? That's Cole Warner's charter. I didn't know you were acquainted."

Her eyebrows climbed. "I don't believe you asked."

"And you're going to crew for him?"

A frisson of distress settled in her midsection. For some reason, the manager had put too much emphasis on the last word. "That's right," she said finally, trying to sound amused. "After all, we're not entering a race competition, so I don't anticipate any trouble." She picked up her receipt and checked her watch. "Now, if you'll excuse me—Cole didn't want me to be late."

It was just as well that she didn't see the scowl that settled on his face as she walked away. Even the cashier looked startled, thinking that Mr. Stacy didn't usually act that way when talking to a guest—especially a guest as lovely as the one who'd just checked out. Her thoughts were brought to an abrupt close when the man rounded on her and snarled, "If you don't have anything to do, I can certainly find some other work for you on this shift."

The woman murmured apologetically and bent over a ledger, but when the manager strode away to his office, it was a good thing he didn't see the gesture she made at his retreating back.

Oblivious to all the byplay, Stephanie walked out of the building onto the wooden deck and then turned onto the main pier. She immediately was surrounded by the organized bedlam, passing yachtsmen and their friends who were watching the loading of stores aboard their chartered vessels, which lined the pier on both sides. Adding to the confusion were the employees pushing carts full of stores and luggage of the embarking guests as well as the greetings of crews aboard returning charters, the latter's sunburned faces and expertise in mooring their luxury crafts making them a breed apart.

Representing another breed entirely was the big pelican watching from his perch atop a vacant buoy, his calm demeanor a graphic contrast to the other inhabitants of the marina. Stephanie slowed her steps to grin at him, thinking he had the right idea toward life. Certainly he was exhibiting more intelligence than the sunburned twosome on a nearby schooner who were arguing loudly about whether or not they needed another bottle of Scotch to take along. She carefully detoured around them and started checking the numbers on the pier. Slip Forty-two was only three more down the line, and her pulse started bounding as soon as she noticed the name "*Bagatelle*" on the stern of a trim white thirty-seven-foot sloop.

There wasn't anyone visible on deck and she stood on the edge of the pier, wondering whether she could safely negotiate the giant step across to the boat. She felt foolish standing there, and yet if she made a misstep, she knew that her sailing career would end abruptly.

Fortunately there was a slight commotion at that moment and a sunburned man wearing a cotton singlet and rumpled trousers emerged from the cabin, followed by her new employer.

The stranger paused long enough to rake her

with a glance that made her feel as if she were wearing a string bikini instead of trim-fitting slacks and blouse.

"Well, little lady, if you're looking for a friend, I'll be glad to volunteer." The man's attempt at humor made her pierce him with a glance that should have withered him on the spot.

"That won't be necessary," Cole Warner said, moving around him and coming to the stern to give her a hand aboard. "I don't believe in sharing. Maybe I should have put out the word," he added in a careless comment over his shoulder. An instant later, when Stephanie was still getting her balance on deck, he put his arms around her and bent his head. "Play along," he muttered under the pretext of nuzzling her ear. "I'll explain soon." Then he slid his mouth along her cheekbone, down to her lips, taking his time over a kiss that left her trembling.

It was the sound of laughter from the other man that brought Stephanie back to the present. "Sorry, mate," he was saying. "I didn't know that the lady was already taken."

Cole kept a firm hand on her waist, as if aware that she needed help to stay erect considering the circumstances. "That just shows that it doesn't pay to make any sudden moves, doesn't it, mate?" The accent he put on the last word showed that, despite his noncommittal tone, he was still posting boundaries. "Stephanie, this is Nevil Taylor, our checkout skipper." He turned to face Taylor. "Stephanie Church, the friend that I told you would be crewing for me this week."

"Oh, I remember," the heavily tanned sailor told him in a mocking tone that still held remnants of an Aussie accent. "What you didn't tell me was that she was a special friend."

"Well, now you know," Cole said.

By then, Stephanie had managed to get her breathing back to a fairly regular cadence. Cole's eyebrows came together warningly as he put a protective arm at her waist. "Let me show you around before we cast off, darling. I put your stuff in the stern cabin, but you can unpack later. Nevil, give us an extra five minutes, will you?"

"I'll give you more than that if you'll toss up a cold one to keep me company," the checkout skipper said, settling on a locker by the tiller.

"One cold one coming up," Cole agreed while steering Stephanie ahead of him down the companionway steps. When she rounded on him at the bottom, he shook his head and put a finger to his lips. Reaching into the refrigerated compartment along one side of the cabin, he pulled out the can of beer. "Here you are," he told Nevil as he went back to the steps again and tossed it up.

"Now, all I have to do is find a bit of shade where I can drink it," the other said, pulling the tab. "I'll go check my mail slot in the office, but I'll be back in ten minutes and then we'd better cast off."

"We'll be ready," Cole assured him, and waited until he'd jumped up on the pier and started down it before turning back to Stephanie.

"I don't know what's going on," she burst out before he could say anything, "but you seem to have the wrong idea about this jaunt. I'm just along for the ride. You get a week's free help while I'm aboard, but that's as far as the benefits go. If you have any other ideas, you can forget them, or I'm leaving right now."

Chapter 2

There was a moment of silence while Cole surveyed her, his jaw tight with annoyance. "Are you quite finished?" he asked finally.

"Well, yes." She shrugged her shoulders, trying to look as if she didn't care about the outcome of her ultimatum. "That's all I have to say."

His expression softened. "I can see where you might have gotten the wrong idea," he said then. "Will you just trust me that it was necessary? It's important that Nevil think we're—old friends."

The way he hesitated before the words let Stephanie translate the phrase immediately into "lovers," and she frowned again.

Cole went on before she could object. "As soon as we leave him at Peter Island at the end of the checkout leg this afternoon, we can forget all that fiction. I'm not any happier about the idea than you are," he told her. "I have no intention of indulging in any short-term affairs —or long ones either—at this particular point in my life."

His tone was so convincing that Stephanie's fears were immediately put to rest. She even found herself resenting the fact that the kiss they'd shared a few minutes earlier hadn't altered his decision in the slightest. Since her own pulse rate was still far from normal, she found his arrogant disclaimer more irritating than the fact that he'd made a pass in the first place.

"Well, will you go along with idea?"

His impatient question brought her abruptly back to reality. "I beg your pardon," she said, looking bewildered.

"I asked if you'd made up your mind," he said, enunciating carefully. "Nevil will be back any minute."

Stephanie rapidly reviewed her options. She still had the chance of the cruise she'd planned on. They were evidently going to be tied up at well-populated islands most nights. From the looks of the cramped quarters in the cabin she'd just seen, it was hardly the place for an impromptu orgy. As a matter of fact, if the darned boat didn't stop bouncing around, Cole might be pressed into service holding her head rather than more sensual parts of her anatomy.

She saw him open his mouth and spoke up quickly before he could utter any more ultimatums. "Okay, I'll go along with the script. Maybe you can fill me in on why this playacting is necessary."

"There isn't time now," he said, standing on the lowest step and looking out toward the pier. "Nevil's evidently finished his beer and is coming back to work. Now don't forget," he said, turning to Stephanie. "We're buddies. If he asks any questions, just follow my lead. Okay?"

She managed a crooked smile. "As long as your lead doesn't involve a shared stateroom, we're in business."

"Don't worry about that," he muttered. "There's barely enough room in that forward stateroom for a good-size midget, so you're safe on that score. And all the rest," he added. "You can relax—stop looking as if you're perched on the rail ready to jump."

"Permission to come aboard, Captain?" Nevil gave them a mock salute and leapt easily onto the stern without waiting for a reply. "Everything sorted out?"

"We're ready to leave if you are," Cole told him. "How do you want to work this?"

"I'll handle the lines until we clear the dock area, you can take care of the wheel, and the little lady"—the checkout skipper sent her a smile that didn't quite reach his eyes—"can just sit over there and look decorative until we get out a bit."

The little-lady remark tempted Stephanie to step on one of his bare feet as she moved in front of him to sit down. Discretion made her stifle the impulse, but she was careful to stay out of his way. He lingered by the cabin when Cole pushed the starter button for the engine.

Stephanie watched all the preparations carefully, aware that she'd probably be pressed into service for the same routine once there were just two of them aboard.

Nevil was watching too, and once Cole switched on the engine, he moved toward the bow, ready to handle the lines there. When Cole nodded to him a minute or two later, he freed them without a wasted motion.

"Let go the stern," Cole told Stephanie. She leaned over to free the line, tossing it up on the pier, where one of the staff had it neatly coiled before they'd hardly pulled away from the dock.

"Is there anything else?" she asked hesitantly, not wanting to disturb Cole as he handled the tricky maneuvering of the big boat in the busy marina waters.

"Not now, thanks. Just stay out of the way," he instructed.

She perched hesitantly on the edge of the cockpit, well beyond where he stood at the wheel, intent on easing the schooner out of the crowded moorage quarters.

"Nevil, take care of the dinghy, will you?" Cole called forward.

"Right." The man moved back to the stern, transferring the dinghy painter to a cleat amidships on the hull after they maneuvered into open water beyond the pier.

Cole increased the speed slightly, but it was a smooth motion on the throttle, Stephanie noted. "I don't understand about the dinghy," she confessed when she deemed it safe to divert his attention. "Aren't they usually off the stern?"

He nodded. "And ours will be later on. This checkout cruise has to do with setting the anchor," he added in a lower tone, watching Nevil pulling in the fenders and stowing them away neatly. When Cole turned his attention back to Stephanie and saw her puzzled expression, he went on, "Setting the anchor involves putting the boat into reverse. If we didn't move the dinghy, the painter could get tangled in the prop and that would be one hell of a mess. Any crew who let that happen would be keelhauled, so take warning."

"It's so hot that I'm not sure it would be any punishment. I'll be very careful," she assured him. "That is, if I'm ever at the wheel."

"Oh, you will be," he said. "Probably in about ten minutes, if I know Nevil."

She made a disdainful grimace. "From the little I've seen of him, I think I'd prefer a good honest keelhauling."

Cole's eyebrows climbed. "What makes you say that?" he asked quietly.

"I don't know. There isn't any reason. Maybe I'd better fall back on the old standby: woman's intuition."

He looked amused. "Don't tell me I've signed on a psychic."

"No such luck," she admitted. "If anything, I probably have negative ESP, if there is such a thing."

"Then I won't check with you for a weather forecast."

"I wouldn't suggest it, unless I've been listening to the radio." She watched as they edged around the end of the marina's breakwater, heading toward Road Harbour. "Is the swell always this bad?"

"This isn't bad." Cole altered their course slightly. "Don't tell me you're the type who gets seasick while we're still in sight of the dock." He frowned and went on, "If you are, you'd better go below and take a motion pill. There's a first-aid box on top of the charts."

"I'm fine," Stephanie told him defensively. "I was just asking a simple question about the weather." She managed a smile as Nevil came toward them and stepped down into the stern cockpit. "Is it time to go to work?"

"That's right." He gestured toward the pea-green hull of an ancient work boat anchored some hundred feet ahead of them. "Now, if you'll take the wheel, sweetheart, we'll let your boss have a go at setting the anchor."

If Stephanie hadn't been aware that her presence on board could be short-lived, she would have reacted to Nevil's choice of words. As it was, she couldn't hide her annoyed expression, but she kept her mouth firmly closed.

"Right." Cole was clearly aware of the undercurrent and shot her a concerned look but merely gestured her to take his place behind the wheel. "Keep it headed into the wind at this speed until I tell you to put the throttle into neutral." He gestured toward the controls at the side of the wheel. "We'll coast a bit until there's no headway. Then, when I lower the anchor, go into reverse." He pointed out the marking on the throttle carefully. "Have you got that?" He must have heard her sudden intake of breath because he lingered long enough to murmur, "Take it easy, you'll do fine," before he left the wheel and made his way toward the bow.

"Anyplace you choose," Nevil called from where he was now watching by the compartment stairs.

Since he was looking at Cole, Stephanie decided to wait and see what other instructions might be forthcoming before she touched the throttle. She was glad that she did because an instant later, Cole called, "Neutral, Stephanie."

Gingerly she grasped the throttle and shoved it to the proper notch.

"Tell him what you did," Nevil barked at her.

She swallowed and then said, "Neutral it is."

"Louder," Nevil commanded. "He's got to hear you."

"Neutral," she shouted back, and felt color wash over her face as Cole looked back startled and then grinned.

Stephanie was so engrossed by the chain of

command that she hadn't observed their diminished speed and was surprised to note suddenly that the sloop was almost dead in the water. She hung on to the wheel so tightly that her fingers felt numb, but at least Nevil couldn't say that she wasn't keeping the bow into the wind. She saw Cole kneel on the deck suddenly and then there was the sound of chain rattling as the anchor went overboard. A moment or two later, the boat started to drift sideways as the anchor hit bottom and almost instantly Cole called, "Reverse it!"

Stephanie took a deep breath and eased the throttle into the proper niche as she called back, "Reverse," and felt the engine take hold.

"Neutral," Cole shouted almost immediately, and Stephanie had the throttle changed before Nevil could turn and look questioningly at her.

"Neutral," she called triumphantly, and responded to Cole's thumbs-up signal with a grin of her own.

"Well, it looks as if you're well and truly anchored," Nevil told her almost grudgingly. "Not bad reaction time. Now you'd better find out what your skipper wants. Sometimes getting under way again in a crowded anchorage can be dicey."

Cole had come back amidships to hear the last of his remarks and he nodded. "Especially if your neighbors are casual about observing unwritten property lines. If you're ready," he told Stephanie, "we'll lift anchor and then head on out to open water. First, you'll put the throttle into forward position and bring the bow back into the wind. When I signal, you'll ease into neutral—"

"I thought you said Stephanie was an experienced crew," Nevil cut in impatiently.

"It's been a while and I did my crewing on small boats, so I told Cole that I'd appreciate going over the drill again." She managed a confident smile for both of them. "After all, I don't want to make any mistakes in a crowded anchorage."

"My feelings exactly," Cole replied, starting forward again. "Just watch my signals."

Stephanie nodded and put the throttle into forward gear, feeling the powerful engine take hold immediately. She took a bearing on the green-hulled work boat and tried to duplicate their heading while watching Cole carefully.

"Neutral," he called back, getting down on the deck to peer over the edge to check on the anchor line.

"Neutral," she confirmed, and slipped the throttle down a notch.

Their progress had just started to slow when a tremendous explosion suddenly erupted in the quiet afternoon air.

Startled, Stephanie clutched the wheel with one hand and shot the throttle into forward gear with the other.

There was an angry shout from the bow, and from the corner of her eye, she saw Cole halfway over the rail and headed for the water.

"What in the hell!" she heard Nevil swear as he knocked her hand from the throttle and shoved the lever back. "Didn't you hear him say neutral?"

"Of course I did," Stephanie defended herself, her knees trembling. "But I didn't plan on being blasted off the map two seconds later." She glanced anxiously toward the bow, where Cole had hauled himself back on deck. "Are you all right?"

She saw him give a terse nod and peer over the side again before he shouted, "Reverse—easy reverse—then neutral again when I signal."

"Can you manage that?" Nevil asked, eyeing her dubiously.

"Of course." She reached for the throttle and did as ordered. "But why reverse?"

"He's trying to straighten out the mess up there. Just do what he says or we'll never get to Peter Island this afternoon, and frankly I'm sick of staying here broiling in the sun." The checkout skipper slumped onto the bench next to the wheel again. "It doesn't do a thing for a hangover."

Stephanie wanted to say that he couldn't blame her for that, too, but contented herself with asking, "What *was* that explosion?"

"They're blasting on the road up there," he said, jerking a thumb toward the hillside rising steeply above the water. "Most of us have gotten used to it over the past weeks."

"It might be nice if they'd let the visitors know," she said, slipping the throttle into neutral at Cole's shout.

"You're supposed to confirm," Nevil told her, "or have you forgotten that, too?"

"Neutral," she called out, but kept her gaze forward so that he wouldn't see the rebellious light in her eyes. If Cole wasn't complaining, she couldn't understand why Nevil was making such a fuss.

Rapid movement on the bow and finally the rattle of chain as Cole hauled the anchor aboard once again kept all her attention after that.

"Okay, let's go," he called back to her. "Head out past the point and then I'll come back and take over. It's too damned hot for any more tests," he added to Nevil. "If I didn't pass on that, I'll arrange to tie up at the pier every night or somebody can come out in a rowboat and perform the necessary."

Nevil uttered a derisive snort. "I'd like to see anybody try it," he muttered to Stephanie before asking, "What do you want done with the dinghy?"

Obviously he was hoping to catch her out, she decided after a quick look at the small boat still bobbing amidships. "Probably Cole will have me move it back to the stern as soon as he takes over the wheel," she said, hoping she sounded properly decisive.

A grudging look of approval passed over Nevil's puffy features. "That's right. Never mind, I'll save you the trouble," he said, starting forward, "but if they start blasting again, try not to head for those rocks on the point."

He could have thought of a hundred topics and managed to avoid that one, Stephanie thought, but she flashed a smile that evaporated as soon as he'd turned his back. She was going to have a sticky-enough time when Cole confronted her without Nevil keeping on about it.

She was still trying to think of a defense when Cole arrived back at the stern and took over the wheel.

"I'm awfully sorry about my mistake back there," she began, deciding she'd better get the topic over with while Nevil was still occupied with lighting a cigarette amidships. "That blasting on the highway caught me by surprise. I honestly wasn't fixing to drown you."

"Relax, I'm still dry. At first I thought you'd decided to try your hand at keelhauling. Then I realized it wasn't all your fault. I jumped a good six inches off the deck at the blast, too. Why don't you go down and make us some instant coffee. My nerves are still frazzled."

Stephanie's anxious face smoothed with relief. "Thanks for letting me off so easily. I'm not too sure about the workings of the galley, but I could brew some real coffee if you'd rather."

Cole shook his head. "Instant will be fine. Coffee isn't the ideal remedy for the jitters, but I'm too much of a northerner to settle for iced tea."

"Right." She moved quickly out of the way as Nevil came back toward them handling the painter for the dinghy so it could be tied off the stern. "Coffee coming up," she said, and headed for the companionway stairs.

It was while she was waiting for the water to boil on the four-burner gas stove that she realized she was pleased that Cole hadn't asked for a cold beer to relax. She'd been on one Sunday pleasure cruise where the powerboat captain had used the day afloat merely as an excuse to get inebriated, and she'd decided that she would go ashore at the first anchorage if Cole was that kind of skipper.

She poured the boiling water in two mugs and then thought she'd better remember her manners. "Would you like some instant coffee?" she asked Nevil, calling up from the bottom of the stairs.

"No way, luv," he announced, adopting a genial tone. "Another can of lager wouldn't go amiss, though, if there's one to spare."

She looked inquiringly at her employer, who nodded and said, "I'm sure you can find one in the cold chest."

Stephanie handed one up a moment later along with Cole's cup of coffee. "Aren't you going to join us?" he wanted to know as she started to turn away.

"In a little bit," she assured him, "but this is a good chance to see what stores we have on hand so I'll know what kind of menus to plan."

"Now, that shows that I needn't have worried about your crew, Captain," Nevil said genially as he opened his beer and took a deep swallow.

"It sounds as if you have a winner in the galley, at least."

Apparently he meant it as a compliment, Stephanie thought from where she stood by the stove. Certainly he was being far more complimentary when she was in the catering department rather than behind the wheel. She frowned slightly as she considered the sparse provisions that were stacked in the cupboards alongside the sink. Even Julia Child would have trouble concocting anything memorable from coffee, tea, peanut butter, cold cereal, a loaf of bread, and some strawberry jam. She walked over to check the cold chest again. Apparently they were well-stocked with cartons of soda, beer, fruit juice, and a gallon of fresh milk. Unfortunately that was where the menu stopped. Cole had completely ignored any vegetables or meat. Unless he planned to have a local pizza-parlor delivery awaiting them when they arrived at Peter Island, it was going to be a thin night for nourishment.

She took another swallow of coffee and immediately felt perspiration break out on her forehead. The two ventilating ports atop the cabin were open, but the air that was coming in was hot. There would be more breeze on deck, and if she could stay in the shade, she might feel better. Certainly the combination of the stuffy cabin and the motion now that they had hit open water wasn't helping her state of mind or stomach.

She swallowed and then abruptly poured the rest of her coffee into the sink drain before making a beeline for the stairs to reach the open deck.

If Cole was aware of the reason for her prompt reappearance topside, he didn't mention it. Other than giving her a casual look as she subsided close to the companionway, he went on with his conversation with Nevil. Apparently they were discussing eating places in the island chain and Nevil was as definite in his opinions on those as sailing a boat.

"For my money, Peter Island is as good as they come," he was saying in authoritative tones. "It isn't easy to secure a reservation anywhere even at this season, so you'd better get on the radio to the hotel as soon as you anchor. That's especially true when you reach Chambers Landing." He paused to look inquisitively at Cole. "If you plan to sail that way again."

"I haven't really made up my mind," Cole said, draining the last swallow from his coffee and nodding his thanks to Stephanie when she got up to relieve him of the cup. "What do you want for an itinerary, mate?"

She had headed for the stairs to put his cup in the sink, but his question made her stop and look over her shoulder. "Well," she tried to remember the names she'd checked on the chart when she arrived, "it would be nice to see Virgin Gorda."

Nevil broke out laughing. "Trust a female,"

he said derisively. "She'll have an infallible knack for knowing the most expensive place five minutes after she arrives."

Stephanie started to protest before encountering Cole's warning look. She subsided then, smiling at Nevil as she said, "I'd hoped to break it to Cole gently. Now he'll really make me work for my passage."

"At least, I'll have an excuse," Cole told her, and then changed the subject by asking Nevil about the weather forecast for the week while Stephanie went into the cabin.

They were still on the topic when she surfaced again, but in the meantime they'd hoisted the mainsail and turned off the engine. Stephanie was able to sit down and relax against the cabin bulkhead, half-closing her eyes to protect them against the sun.

In reality, it gave her a fine opportunity to stare at Cole while his attention was on Nevil or keeping the sail trimmed in the freshening wind.

From his relaxed stance behind the wheel, she could tell that he was very much in control of the situation. At least, she'd been hired by a competent skipper, she thought with satisfaction, mentally alert as well as physically pleasing. Even when blown by the wind, his dark hair was thick and healthy-looking. And he already had a tan that would probably be almost a teak shade by the end of their trip. She hadn't thought that gray eyes could be so piercing, but they were, and she closed her own when his gaze momentarily swung to rest on her. When she opened them again, he had turned to answer a question Nevil had put to him.

It was amazing how different the two men were, she thought dispassionately. The checkout skipper was only an inch or so short of six feet, but where Cole was tall and rangy, Nevil looked like a TV ad for the neighborhood bodybuilding club. Which was probably one reason he adopted that tank top, she observed: it showed his powerful shoulders and biceps to the best advantage. And if anybody did happen to overlook them, she was sure that he'd find an opportunity to flex his muscles. His waistline wasn't quite so trim, though, and there were definite lines of dissipation around his eyes and mouth. Even his deeply tanned skin couldn't hide them or the thick shock of fair hair that flopped onto his forehead and was long enough to curl over his collar—if he'd been wearing a collar.

"You didn't mention you were going to be back in this part of the world the last time I talked to you," he was saying to Cole.

"That's because I didn't know I'd get some extra vacation." Cole squinted as he checked the mainsail. "As soon as I found out, I phoned to see if there was a charter available."

"And crew?" Nevil added, sending a quick look in Stephanie's direction.

"Ah, yes. That's where I was lucky this time. Stephanie was an added bonus."

"So it would seem," Nevil commented in a wry tone. "A remarkable coincidence."

"Not really. I'd told her how great the sailing was down here when I got home the first time. Remember, Steff? It was at that cruise-line publicity thing, wasn't it?"

She managed to keep her voice equally casual when she replied. "I can't remember. Either there or that brunch the Morgans gave. Why? Does it matter?"

He bestowed an approving smile on her. "Not to me, darling. You're here now, and that's all that counts."

Nevil didn't appear cheered by their dialogue. "You'd better alter your course to starboard if you want to head for the main Peter Island harbor. I gather that's where you plan to spend tonight."

"That's it. We'd run out of daylight if we headed for anyplace else by now. Besides, it will be a good place to do our own shakedown cruise before we get too far from the home marina."

"You've never sailed together before, then?" Nevil asked.

Stephanie kept her eyes half-closed, letting Cole handle the rest of their story. "Nope," he said briefly, "but I don't think we'll have any trouble."

"Probably not," Nevil admitted. "William Stacy, the manager at the marina, was surprised to hear that you two were old friends. He said that you didn't give any indication of it when you met each other in his office this morning. As a matter of fact, your lady was still trying to find an available charter then."

"That's because we'd had a little misunderstanding. It's all cleared up now, isn't it, love?" Cole asked.

His words were casual but the steely undertone made Stephanie's eyes widen. "Of course, darling." She managed to bat her lashes in the approved fashion as she flashed a bright smile up at him. "I was just being silly. It wasn't your fault that we couldn't fly down here together. And even if I had found another berth," she went on, to Nevil, "I certainly would have changed my plans once Cole explained everything."

"I see." Nevil gave her a mocking salute. "When I return to the marina, I'll have to tell William that everything has been settled nicely. He can report back to your firm that we've done our part."

"That won't be necessary," Stephanie was going to say, and then subsided at Cole's sudden frown. She reached for her brimmed hat and took refuge beneath it. "If I'm not needed, I'll try to get a short nap before we dock. I still must be suffering from jet lag." Thank God for airplanes, she thought as Nevil reluctantly turned his attention back to boating. She wondered how many times jet lag had been used as an excuse in people's lives, and then she found her eyelids getting heavier as the warm tropical breeze caressed her face.

Cole's voice penetrated her consciousness later, interrupting a dream that had Nevil trailing behind the sloop in place of the dinghy. She blinked and sat up, still more than half asleep. "What did you say?" she asked, barely managing to cover a yawn with the back of her hand.

"I said," he repeated in a tone that made her sit up even straighter, "that you'd better wake up to handle the wheel. We're almost at the harbor."

"We can't be!" Stephanie turned to peer toward the bow and was amazed to see the distinctive outline of Peter Island looming in front of them. "Good Lord, I had no idea."

"I didn't think you did." Cole's tone showed that he wasn't going to be patient much longer. "Just come and take the wheel, will you?"

"Yes, of course." She scrambled toward him and almost fell flat when she found her foot was still asleep. "I'm sorry," she said, nearly lurching into Nevil's lap as he watched in amusement.

"The motion bothering you?" he asked as she reached the wheel.

"No, it's . . ." Suddenly she realized she'd sound like a fool if she told the truth. "Probably I'll get used to it in time. What course do I steer?" she asked Cole as he stood back to let her sidle in front of him.

"Just around the end of the breakwater," he said, gesturing ahead of them. "I'll lower the mainsail and we'll go in under power. Okay?"

She nodded, holding on to the wheel and

trying to ignore the prickly feeling in her foot, which she kept firmly planted on deck. Determined to do her job properly, she wasn't going to look like a flamingo yard decoration until the circulation sorted itself out.

"Right. Let's go under power from now on," Cole called. "Start the engine but keep it below fifteen hundred rpm."

She nodded and reached down to push the button, unaware that she'd been holding her breath until the sound of the motor responded immediately. Carefully she moved the throttle until the tachometer read just under fifteen hundred.

A few minutes later, Cole had the mainsail down. Nevil moved alongside the mast to assist getting the dacron neatly rolled on the boom until Cole had it secured with bungee cords.

The checkout skipper came back to perch alongside the wheel then as Cole moved forward to the bow, checking the anchor lines. "I hope you kept your eyes open," Nevil said to Stephanie. "You may have to help out in that procedure when there's just the two of you. Not that he couldn't handle it alone, but sometimes time is a factor."

She took a deep breath and then said, "I can manage."

"Good." Nevil reached for a battered pack of cigarettes and selected one, remembering belatedly to offer the pack in her direction.

"No, thanks. I don't smoke."

"You Americans are so pure these days," he commented, cupping his hands to shield the match. "One good thing about it, though: we don't find nearly as many cigarette burns after the charters." He moved out of the way as Cole came back to the stern.

"Take it more to starboard," Cole told Stephanie after another look over the bow. "Give the end of the breakwater plenty of room, as well as that fifty-one-footer over there."

"A vessel on the port tack shall keep out of the way of a close-hauled vessel on the starboard tack," she murmured.

"What's that?" Cole asked.

"Just going over the rules of the road," she told him. "The most important is, don't argue if they're a lot bigger."

"I don't think you'll come up against any ocean-going freighters in these waters," Nevil told her in some amusement. "The interisland ferries constitute most of the local traffic." He looked at his watch and nodded approvingly. "It looks as if I'll be in good time to catch the last one back to Road Town."

"Any special place in Sprat Bay that you'd suggest for anchoring?" Cole asked, surveying the shoreline ahead of them.

Nevil shook his head. "It's all the same. You might experience a surge here overnight, so you'll have to make provision for it with your lines."

Cole nodded as he squinted across the water. "I remember reading about that, but thanks for mentioning it. Head for that clump of shrubbery up there," he instructed Stephanie. "Be ready to cut the motor when I tell you."

"And I wouldn't advise you to make any mistakes this time," Nevil said to Stephanie in a low tone as soon as Cole was beyond hearing. "If you run aground here, there are apt to be two of us on that ferry back to Road Town tonight."

Stephanie nodded grimly, her fingers clutching the wheel tightly. She had no idea of the depth at that point, but presumably Cole did, since she'd seen a chart for the waters of Peter Island spread out in the cabin when she'd been making coffee.

At that moment, Cole yelled, "Put it in neutral."

Stephanie had gripped the throttle almost before he'd finished speaking and called back, "Neutral it is."

The sloop's speed went down slowly in the calm water inside the breakwater. Stephanie was vaguely aware of steep-roofed dwellings to her left along with two work boats at the long pier. Fortunately there weren't any other sloops anchored nearby for her to worry about, but she did cast an anxious eye overboard hoping that the depth was safe.

By then, they were almost dead in the water with just the slightest motion from the swells. Suddenly she saw Cole bend down and release the anchor—hearing the rattle of the chain an instant later. He watched its progress and then turned toward the stern to call out, "Reverse—slowly."

Even without his emphasis on that word, Stephanie would have understood. "Reverse," she called back, and reached for the throttle again.

"Get ready to cut your power. Just the way you did in our practice drill," Nevil commanded, watching her carefully.

She nodded and had barely felt the tug of the anchor line before Cole shouted, "Cut engine."

"Engine out," she confirmed, her finger stabbing the button.

Cole stayed in the bow a moment longer before coming back to the stern again, saying, "I may put out a second anchor if it gets crowded in here later on."

"Not a bad idea." Nevil stood up and stretched. "Well, I guess you two are safe to send out on your own. As long as there aren't any blasting crews around."

Very funny, Stephanie thought to herself. Aloud, she merely said, "I'll make sure to check in the morning."

Nevil didn't bother to reply to that, instead glancing at his watch again to say, "Well, I might as well go ashore and have words with a friend of mine at the yacht club before the ferry comes in." He looked at Cole. "Are the two of you going ashore now or . . ." His voice trailed off.

"I'll just take you and then come back. You probably would like a chance to unpack, wouldn't you?" Cole asked, turning to Stephanie.

"If this is a good time," she agreed.

"Then I'll take off," Nevil said, leaning over the stern to catch the painter and start pulling the dinghy alongside.

Cole bent over the storage bin beside the wheel, reaching in for the boarding ladder, which he secured amidships. Stephanie watched Nevil bring the dinghy around before deciding they didn't need her assistance. She thought about asking Cole if he planned on coming right back, and then decided that sounded too much like a possessive spouse. She settled for saying casually to Nevil, "It was nice to have met you. Thanks for all your help."

"No trouble," he said. "If you relax a little bit, you should manage to get through the week."

Which was certainly damning with faint praise, she thought as she disappeared down the stairs into the cabin.

She stayed away from the porthole while she heard them boarding the dinghy until the motor was started on the small craft. After that, she pressed her nose against the glass above the sink in the galley to watch the two men as they headed for the long pier the *Bagatelle* had skirted coming into the harbor. Stephanie let her glance wander, taking in the steep A-framed dwellings overlooking the water and the lush green vegetation on the hillside. There was nothing like glorious blue sky, white clouds, and palm trees as the backdrop for a vacation paradise, she thought happily, and then remembered she'd better unpack before Cole returned.

Not that there was much room to spread out, she discovered a little later as she surveyed her two pieces of luggage, which took up a good half of the triangular stern cabin she'd been allotted. There wasn't room to stand up straight either, she found out when she pulled her case down on the mattress. Fortunately there was a small fan mounted on the side wall and she turned it on full force to move the hot air around. The fan responded, but it also made an unpleasant whine, which showed that the motor needed an overhaul. She frowned and decided to put that on a list of "things to check out" later.

There were clean sheets already on the bed and extra linen stored immediately to her left. On reaching for a pillow from the pile, she discovered it was as warm as if it had just been resting on a heat register. She frowned and felt the storage locker, only to burst out laughing. The head of her bed was apparently right over the engine! Something to be desired if they'd been cruising a Minnesota lake in midwinter; in the BVI during late spring it promised very warm nights. Thank God for the fan, she thought, even though it sounded as if some of its innards were missing. At least she wouldn't have to bother with blankets, she concluded, and shoved them out of reach at the foot of her bed.

By sitting on the mattress, she was able to partially unpack her suitcase, storing two dresses and a jacket in the small locker. Shorts, slacks, and tops she left in the case before she shoved it under the bunk. All that was left was to take her toiletries bag and put it on the counter of the stern head. She didn't have to worry about taking up too much space in there, for she'd discovered that Cole had his own facilities adjoining the stateroom in the bow.

Once inside, she noticed the intricate instructions on the door for the use of the plumbing. Now was as good a time as any to experiment. There weren't going to be many secrets aboard, she thought after starting at the top of the rules sheet.

By following them carefully, she managed to accomplish her aim, but the pumping phase was loud enough to disturb a South American sloth. Hardly discreet either—especially if she had to stumble into the facilities in the middle of the night. On the other hand, maybe Cole was a heavy sleeper, she told herself, and then grinned as she realized that the pumping apparatus in Cole's bathroom was probably as noisy as hers. So much for life afloat, she thought, and shrugged before going back to the galley.

She'd meant to ask Cole about dinner preparations earlier, but somehow she hadn't wanted to discuss their grocery supply in front of Nevil. On the other hand, if she stayed down in the hot cabin much longer, she wouldn't have to bother about dinner at all. Cole was right! She should have taken a motion pill earlier on. The only good thing about her queasiness was that it disappeared when she stayed on deck.

That was where Cole found her a little later when he brought the dinghy around the bow of the *Bagatelle* and tossed up the painter once he was positioned under the boarding ladder amidships. He nodded approvingly as she secured the line before he came aboard.

"I'm happy to see that you're keeping your eyes open," he commented, leading the way back to the stern. "Did you finish unpacking?"

She nodded. "I also checked out the stores. They're a little thin," she began diplomatically, and paused when he burst out laughing.

"And you're wondering if you should have brought along some trail rations to tide you over," he said.

The thought of smoke-dried jerky didn't do much for her stomach even in the fresh air. "Not really," she told him. "I just didn't know what you had in mind for me to do in the galley."

"The only thing I had in mind was to eat dinner ashore every night," he told her, sobering abruptly. "There may be a time later on when it won't be convenient, but we'll wait and see. And as far as lunch goes tomorrow, we can either patronize a delicatessen at the anchorage on Virgin Gorda or there's a good pub not far from the marina. Incidentally you'll have to change for dinner at the hotel tonight," he added. "They don't approve of casual sailing attire in the dining room. You did bring along a dress, didn't you? Or something that will pass muster with the maître d'?"

"Well, yes." Stephanie looked at him dubiously, wondering if he expected her to accompany him or whether she was on her own.

Before she could ask, he nodded and started for the cabin stairs. "Right. I made our dinner reservation for seven-thirty. That will give me time for a swim in Deadman's Bay. On the other side of the island," he added impatiently, seeing her puzzled expression. "Or you can check out the hotel gift shop. At any rate, the dinghy's leaving in about ten minutes, so you'll have to make up your mind."

With that pronouncement, he disappeared down the stairs. A moment later, she heard the slamming of the forward cabin door. So much for the beginning of a beautiful friendship, Stephanie thought. At least she was invited to share his table for dinner, which wasn't to be sneezed at. Maybe under the more civilized conditions at the hotel, she could find out why Cole was taking this cruise. One thing did seem sure: he wasn't anxious for her company during his afternoon swim. That meant she'd better pretend a great desire to explore the gift shop. It certainly sounded better than simply sunning herself aboard while waiting for time to pass. And it also would do her stomach a world of good to part company with life afloat even for a little while.

She was ready with her shoulder bag and sunglasses when Cole came back on deck. Her glance roamed over his tanned torso, which seemed more formidable than ever in a brief pair of navy-blue swim trunks and a thigh-length white toweling robe. A pair of well-worn leather sandals completed the outfit. She felt her cheeks redden when he intercepted her survey.

"I take it that you've opted out on a swim," he said, letting his own gaze wander over her figure, still attired in the same outfit she'd worn since coming aboard.

"A gift shop sounds like fun," she said as she shoved her sunglasses on her nose and started for the boarding ladder. "Shall I go first?" she asked, gesturing toward the bobbing dinghy.

"Can you manage?" His tone was dry.

"Certainly."

Fortunately she scrambled down and subsided onto the middle seat of the tiny craft without incident. She glanced up to see Cole surveying her with an enigmatic smile, and then he undid the painter and came down to the stern. An instant later, he'd started the motor and was heading toward the long pier where an interisland ferry was just then docking.

"Is that the one our friend Nevil is taking back to Road Town?" Stephanie asked, jerking her head toward it.

"That's it," Cole confirmed. "Last one for the day—or so Nevil says. He was pretty relaxed about catching it. For a while this afternoon, I was afraid we were going to have an overnight guest."

Stephanie thought about the cramped quarters down below and shuddered. Despite what naval architects claimed and salesmen promised, only very good friends indeed should occupy the *Bagatelle* overnight.

Cole evidently had been watching her changing expression. "You don't look as if you thought much of that idea," he said, throttling down the motor so he could talk in a normal tone as they cruised across the harbor.

Stephanie watched him take the ferry's wake on the quarter bow so she remained unscathed, although a little spray would have felt good in the late-afternoon heat.

"Well, do you?"

She came back to the present abruptly. "I'm sorry. Do I what?"

"I was trying to find out what you thought of Nevil," he said dryly. "In a diplomatic way."

"Let's say that I'm sure he knows boats from A to Z, but I'm just as happy he's getting on that one right now," she said, gesturing toward the small ferry, which was tied up at the end of the pier by then. "I hope I'm not maligning a friend of yours," she added an instant later.

"Not at all. I've just met him once before. When I was down here earlier," Cole said. "He was propping up the bar at a hotel on Gorda Sound and buying drinks all around."

"I wouldn't think he'd have that much money to spend."

"Umm. The same thought occurred to me." Cole deftly turned the dinghy to the other end of the pier close to shore, where a small wooden landing stage bobbed next to the pilings.

Stephanie surveyed it with some trepidation, noting that she'd have to scale almost a three-foot barrier to get on the pier beyond. It was okay with the clothes she had on, but dressed for dinner later on, it could pose a problem. Especially if she had to flop onto it like a beached porpoise.

She decided to face that problem when it arose and let Cole handle securing the dinghy when they came alongside, since he didn't seem to expect anything from her. She watched closely how he did it, though, so that she could take over when they came in for dinner later.

"Looks as if Nevil is on his way," Cole commented a little later when they were on the landing platform. "That ferry certainly doesn't waste any time," he added as the craft headed for open water with a sudden roar that reverberated in the quiet air of Sprat Bay. Then, noticing that Stephanie was eyeing the distance up to the pier, he said, "Hold on. I'll give you a boost."

He did it effortlessly. Probably he managed to leap tennis nets with a single bound too, Stephanie thought jealously. Before she could dwell on it, he'd bent down and clasped her under the arms to swing her up beside him. Then he was striding down the pier toward the shore, obviously expecting her to keep up with him. "We'd better set a time to meet," he said, checking the watch on his wrist. "How about forty-five minutes back at the dinghy? Will that give you enough leeway?"

"Fine, thanks," she replied, trying not to sound breathless from their pace.

"Okay, you take the path to the left," he directed when they reached the shore end of the pier. "Most of the amenities are up at the top over there. See you later."

With that laconic comment, Stephanie watched him stride along another path marked with a sign saying BEACH that led straight up the gentle hill in front of them.

At that moment, a cool ocean dip sounded much more inviting than killing time in the gift shop. On the other hand, she hadn't been invited to share that particular bit of ocean. She brushed a strand of hair back from her cheek and started slowly up the path past attractive landscaping of the hotel buildings.

The gift shop was in one of the outer wings of the elegant low structure, and Stephanie discovered immediately that it wasn't stocked with the usual tourist gimcrackery, but expensive items that made her wish she didn't have to consider her budget. At any rate, if she were extravagant, it had best be on the way to the airport, her return ticket clutched firmly in her hand.

She wandered outside again finally and walked up to the huge outdoor pool. Its contemporary design fitted with the decor of the lobby, allowing an indoor-outdoor scheme that was especially attractive. No wonder Cole had suggested best bib-and-tucker for dinner in such surroundings! Just a quick glance at the guests she'd seen roaming the grounds confirmed his suggestion.

She didn't feel like settling into one of the chairs in the attractive lobby, nor baking in the sun on a lounger near the pool. Frowning, she lingered by a display of hotel brochures while she considered her options.

Even though she didn't plan to swim, there was nothing to prevent her from following the path that Cole had taken over the hill. If she happened to encounter him, she could always say that she needed a brisk walk after the confines of the *Bagatelle*.

She pushed her sunglasses more firmly on her nose and started retracing her route down the path until she came to the fork and turned up the hill. Her pace slowed after the first twenty feet, for the grade was steep and the sun still burned on her back despite the late-afternoon hour. There was considerable greenery at either side of the wide tract but not enough tall palms to provide much shade. That was the only fault she could find with her surroundings, since every inch of the resort grounds seemed to be manicured. There were a few turnings from the path with numbers on small signs and a warning that the access was private. Evidently the hotel guests were paying for solitude and expected to get it.

A few feet farther and Stephanie reached the ridge. She drew a sudden breath of delight at the vista spread below her.

It was a gorgeous curve of beach with white sand and breakers of azure water almost too beautiful to be believed. The cove was bounded a mile or so out in the water by Dead Chest Island, if her memory of the chart aboard the sloop served her right.

Stephanie wondered why in the world she hadn't worn a swimsuit under her clothes so that she could take advantage of those gentle breakers foaming onto the deserted beach.

And it was deserted, she decided, taking another look at the raked sand. Unless Cole was sitting under one of the palms farther down, or resting near a clump of sea grape, which seem to edge the path all the way along.

She sighed and made her way down to the damp sand; if she couldn't go swimming, at least she could wade in the cool water. A minute or so later, her shoes were dangling from her fingers as she started down the beach on the edge of the waves.

After a few feet, she ventured slightly deeper into the water in hopes of glimpsing some of the brightly colored tropical fish for which the islands were renowned. Perhaps if she could investigate around some rocks, she thought later after a fruitless search. There was a formation down the beach near the water's edge. She squinted as she checked the location and then a frown creased her forehead as she suddenly noticed two figures seated on the dry sand, almost camouflaged by the heavy thicket of sea grape around them.

Even at a distance, she recognized Cole's terry-cloth jacket and she hurriedly moved out of the water, not pausing until she was almost back on the path. Then she sat down at the base of a palm, brushing the sand from her damp feet. She grimaced as she put on her sandals again, trying to ignore the grit as she stood up and considered her next move.

Obviously the smart thing would be to return to the landing stage, but there was still fifteen minutes before their meeting time and it would be nice to see whom Cole had met. From her quick glance, it appeared to be a man, but she wasn't sure. It would make more sense if it were a woman. Then Cole would have had a logical excuse for not wanting two females on his hands.

Stephanie gave an exasperated sigh and started down the path toward the two of them as she had known she'd do all along. At least she could get reasonably close and satisfy her curiosity without Cole ever knowing.

Fortunately there weren't any other guests abroad at that moment, so she didn't have to suffer raised eyebrows when she sought the very edge of the trail, trying to walk noiselessly on the hard-baked surface.

The shrubbery thickened on the ocean side of the path as she progressed along the private beach. There were one or two cabañas complete with empty loungers, showing that occasionally the hotel guests used the wide beach instead of their private pools or the huge one next to the lobby.

Stephanie's steps slowed as she peered through the foliage and caught a glimpse of movement on the sand. Evidently Cole and his friend were getting ready to leave. "Damn," she whispered in an undertone, and decided to risk another glance before beating a retreat along the walkway or hiding in the shrubbery herself until they were out of sight.

That was the last conscious thought she had, because a split second later she received a violent shove that catapulted her headfirst into the trunk of a tall palm tree growing at the edge of the path. There was an instant of sheer terror, followed by an excruciating flash of pain before an ominous darkness enveloped her like a shroud and stayed there.

Chapter 3

The water felt wonderfully cool, Stephanie thought when she struggled back to consciousness. It was a stupid shower, though, because a constant stream kept running in her ears. She moved her head to avoid it and then moaned with pain. "Dear God," she said, squinting as she tried to sit upright and cope with a throbbing headache that made her forget all about wet ears. By making an effort to focus, she discovered she was still on the beach but stretched on a lounger in one of the cabañas she'd noticed earlier. She put up a hand and scowled as she discovered a rising lump at one side of her forehead.

Then she became conscious of an approaching figure and a familiar voice saying, "What in the devil are you trying to do?"

"I am trying," she said in freezing tones, "to discover if my head is still attached to my neck." Then suddenly sighting the dripping towel he was holding in front of him, she felt her wet cheek. "It was you," she accused. "My ear is full of water and I'm—I'm all wet," she added as she glanced down her front.

"You were also *non compos mentis*." Cole sounded just as irritable. "What did you expect me to do? I was just about to leave you here and make a mad dash to the hotel for a doctor. Why didn't you tell me you were feeling bad earlier on?" He absently rubbed his face with the wet towel and then frowned as water dripped down his cheek.

A sudden surge of anger made Stephanie's head throb even more. "Because I wasn't feeling bad," she told him in a dangerous level voice. "At least not until somebody gave me an almighty shove into that miserable palm tree." She gestured in the general direction. "I don't know what happened after that."

"I do," he answered grimly. "I came along and found you sprawled out cold in the sand. My God! I almost collapsed on top of you from the shock. You're sure somebody shoved you?"

"Of course I am. There's nothing wrong with the inside of my head." She explored the lump at her temple with a careful touch. "I'll probably have a black eye in the morning."

He nodded and started wringing out his towel. "I take it you don't want any more of the cold-water treatment."

"Thanks—but no thanks."

"Okay." He looked up and down the deserted beach, frowning. "I should still go up to the hotel and see if there's a doctor or nurse on duty."

"And leave me here alone?" She started to shake her head and then stopped abruptly, wincing at the pain. "No way. I'll be okay once I take some aspirin and can rest awhile. Honestly," she added when he still didn't respond.

"Well, we can go back to the landing stage and see how you feel," he temporized finally. "Are you able to walk?"

"There's only one way to find out." She swung her legs over the edge of the lounger and stood up. There was an instant when the landscape refused to stay still, but then it obediently steadied. "I'm okay."

For the first time, he gave her a reluctant smile. "That's good. I'm not sure I could manage more than a couple hundred yards unless I threw you over my shoulder in a fireman's carry, and that wouldn't help your head."

"Don't even think about it." She accepted his arm around her waist thankfully and thought how nice it was to feel his strong body shored up against her.

The walk up the hill wasn't as bad as Stephanie had feared. Cole shortened his stride so that it was easy for her to keep alongside, and in his firm clasp she didn't have to worry about her dizziness recurring. When they came to the fork in the path, he surprised her by turning up toward the hotel.

"Where are you going?" she asked, stiffening in his grasp.

"To find the nearest nurse or doctor or whatever," he told her in a tone that didn't brook further questioning. "I want somebody to take a look at that lump on your head. If necessary, we can have emergency help flown over from Road Town."

Stephanie's first instinct was to protest, but then she decided against it. After all, she'd been recruited as a crew—she couldn't blame Cole for wanting to make sure she could pull her weight in the days to come.

Five minutes later he was lowering her onto an upholstered chair at the edge of the lobby. "Wait here," he instructed before striding toward the desk. After a short interval, he was back, holding out a hand to help her up. "We're in luck," he said tersely. "They have a retired doctor who's nearby. We're to wait in their dispensary just down the hall there."

The small first-aid room was immaculate, and Stephanie had barely perched on a metal chair before a gray-haired man carrying a black bag appeared.

"I'm Doctor Clark," he said briskly. "I hear you've been keeping company with a palm tree."

"I didn't plan it that way," Stephanie said, reassured by his kind expression. "And I'm really okay."

"You probably are, but we'll just make sure," the doctor told her. "There's no need to spoil your holiday when a few pills might help things along."

"I'll be waiting outside," Cole announced. "I want to have a word with the manager."

The examination with the doctor didn't take long, but Stephanie wasn't happy when he finally patted her on the shoulder and said he'd be right back, closing the door firmly behind him when he left the room.

Five minutes later, it was Cole who reappeared and assisted her to her feet. "We've had a small change of plans," he told her, not mincing his words. "The doctor wants you to have a night of uninterrupted rest and give that headache a chance to fade out. The manager has arranged for a room."

"But I don't want to be left here," Stephanie protested. "Whoever shoved me might decide to come back and improve his aim."

"I know. That's why I'm staying with you. The manager has beefed up security on the grounds."

"Why can't we sleep aboard the *Bagatelle* the way we planned?"

"That stateroom isn't the first or last word in comfort," Cole told her, leading her out into the lobby before turning down a corridor at the far end. A little farther on, he pulled a key from his pocket and unlocked a door. "Here you are. Don't get used to the luxury, though, or I'll never get you back aboard."

Stephanie went in to find a spacious bedroom decorated in cool tones of silver and orchid. An archway by the side of the big double bed led into a small sitting room. It was complete with sofa and upholstered chairs in white linen above an amethyst carpet. The windows of both rooms overlooked a wonderful tropical garden edged by palms.

"It's gorgeous," Stephanie said, wishing her head wasn't aching so she could enjoy the palatial surroundings. "Did you have to mortgage your soul for a night's stay?"

"Not quite." He urged her toward the edge of the bed and watched her sit down on it. "The manager's a very decent sort. After hearing what happened, he probably would have offered the bridal suite or anything we wanted." Cole was fishing in his pocket and pulled out a vial of pills. "You're to take two of these and then go to bed—either in that order or vice versa. Maybe it would be safer to get in bed first. I got the feeling from what the doctor said that they're apt to make you a little weak in the knees."

"But I don't have pajamas or anything," she started to say, and broke off when she saw him shake his head.

"Sorry. There's no time for the gracious-living bit. Either you sleep in your skivvies or *au naturel*. Right now I'm going in the bathroom to get some water so you can take the pills. If you're not in bed when I come back, I'll make sure that you get there pronto."

Stephanie opened her mouth to protest his high-handedness and found herself looking at his back as he disappeared into the adjoining bath. "Honestly," she fumed, but struggled out of clothes as ordered. Her nylon bikini briefs and bra were barely decent, but there wasn't much she could do about it. She slid beneath the sheet just as the bathroom door opened again.

"Good. I'm glad that you've learned how to follow orders," Cole said, emerging with the pills in one hand and a glass of water in the other.

Stephanie couldn't think of an acceptable answer to that in her present state. She was aware there was a great deal of bare skin showing between the two of them; Cole's terry-cloth jacket was barely midthigh. She hoisted the sheet under her arms to try to keep a semblance of dignity. However, she might as well have been a flounder on a platter for all that Cole's expression revealed. Since her head was pounding at that particular moment, she decided to resent his blank expression later and reached for the pills he was offering.

After she swallowed them, she did remember something that had been bothering her. "There's only one bed in this suite," she said, sounding like a tour guide enumerating the amenities. That was acceptable, she told herself, since her real desire was to know where in hell he planned to sleep.

"That's right." His tone was unruffled. "One

double bed, one sofa, two baths, one balcony. I think two people can struggle along with that."

"I guess so." A strange lethargy was starting to creep over Stephanie. And it wasn't her knees that it was affecting—it was her eyelids. They were getting heavier by the second. Suddenly she decided to lay her cards on the table while she still could. "You *will* stay here, please. I know that I'm probab—probab"—the word was too much and she tried another—"silly, but I'm scared."

"It's okay. I'm staying. Relax."

Stephanie nodded, but even that was an effort. The other question she meant to ask—about exactly where he was going to stay—was too much of an effort. The easiest thing was simply to close her eyes—so, she did.

Cole stared down at her pale cheeks, which were at such variance with the ugly abrasion at her hairline, and shook his head silently. This was one eventuality that he hadn't considered. Unfortunately now it was too late to change plans and he had the feeling that Stephanie would react in no uncertain manner if he even tried. Even as he stared down at her, she turned restlessly in the bed, pushing the sheet down to her waist. Cole rubbed the back of his neck, wondering whether to follow his instincts or let well enough alone. "What the hell," he muttered, and turned to the phone on the bedside table.

It was dark when Stephanie awoke hours later. Someone had left the light on in her bath and the door ajar so she was able to see that the bedroom was empty, although some of Cole's gear was on the bureau against the wall. Then, as she rubbed her aching head, she noticed light under the louvered doors off the sitting room.

On the verge of calling out to Cole, she decided to check and see who was there herself. She swung her feet to the carpet before stopping to glance down at the pale-yellow satin sleep shirt that ended just above her knees. Then she moved uncertainly over to the mirror above the dressing table and stared at her dim reflection. It was a very pretty sleep shirt, with a lacy bodice and delicate cap sleeves. The only bad thing was that her face didn't warrant such elegance. Her suspicion as to how she came to be wearing it made her aching head throb even more, and she moaned softly.

There was a sudden thud in the other room and then the louvered doors were flung open to reveal Cole's tense form. "What in the hell are you doing out of bed?" he wanted to know, coming to put a supportive arm around her shoulders.

Stephanie just had time to notice that he was only wearing dark-blue pajama bottoms before she defended herself. "I got up to find the bathroom."

"The last time I looked, it was over there behind you," he said sardonically, turning her in that direction and walking her toward the door. "But it's just as well you're awake. You're

supposed to have some more pills about now."
When she hesitated, he shoved her gently toward
the open door. "I'll have them ready for you
when you come out. If you can manage alone,"
he finished after inspecting her drawn features.

"I'm fine," she said hurriedly.

"Sure and I'm the first admiral of the Queen's
navy. Never mind, just don't lock the door. If I
hear a body falling, I want a clear field for the
rescue."

She managed a shaky smile. "I promise—you'll
be the first to know."

An instant or two later, when she surveyed
her reflection in the mirror over the basin, she
could see why he was worried. The bruise on
her forehead made her look like the survivor of
an inner-city street fight. The only attractive
part of the picture was the satin sleep shirt,
which wasn't the kind ever found on end-of-the-
month sales. Stephanie took a minute to finger it
appreciatively before noting that the briefs and
bra she had been wearing were neatly hung on a
pullout clothesline over the tub.

An impatient knock on the door behind her
accompanied Cole's irritable "Are you all right
in there?"

"I'm fine," she assured him, and then added,
"I'll be out in a minute."

It was closer to five minutes when she emerged,
to find him hovering by the bed table. "You
stretched it a little fine," he said dispassionately
after another masculine survey that didn't miss

an inch from her ankles to her bruised head. "The doctor prescribed rest—and I don't want a first mate with a headache tomorrow." He waited long enough for her to settle back in bed before tipping two more pills into her palm and presenting the glass of water. After making sure that she swallowed the medicine, he relented enough to ask, "Anything else you need?"

Stephanie pursed her lips and thought about it. "A steak doesn't sound bad," she said finally, surprised to find that she meant it.

He grinned and reached over to turn out the light by the head of her bed. "Sorry. You'll have to settle for a poached egg and toast at breakfast if you feel like it then."

It was while she was considering the menu selection that her eyelids came down again. That time, she didn't even hear him leave the room.

Chapter 4

There was pale sunlight edging the draperies when Stephanie surfaced again. Her first thought was how much better she felt. Even the bump on her forehead wasn't throbbing, she decided happily and reached up to check it out. On the way, her fingers encountered a warm, solid object that made her blink in surprise. Then, finally focusing on Cole's bare shoulder just a whisper away, she drew a sharp breath. She tried to sit up to survey the situation more accurately but she discovered his arm was resting across her waist, effectively pinning her flat on the mattress.

She opened her lips to protest and then reconsidered. She could see he was sound asleep, face down on his pillow. Probably the barrier wasn't intentional on his part; he'd evidently turned onto his stomach, and his arm had merely flopped over her still form.

Which wasn't surprising, Stephanie discovered with growing chagrin as she saw that she was over the middle of the bed, relegating Cole to the very edge of the mattress.

She lay quietly on her pillow, thinking about it. His presence must have been a desperation move, since he really wasn't in the bed—merely atop it. It looked as if there'd even been a struggle for the only comforter, because he'd anchored the edge of it under his knee.

Her guilt intensified as she discovered that a good three-quarters of the cover was on her side of the bed beyond his reach.

Without doubt, her best tactic would be retreat—as soon as possible, before he stirred.

She almost made it. She'd lifted his wrist in a gentle grip and was sliding toward the far side of the mattress when he blinked and then sat up abruptly.

"What's going on?" he growled.

He was obviously too wide awake for her to make soothing noises, so she dropped all pretense. "I'm going to get up," she said, suiting her action to the words.

"Good. Maybe I can finally have some of the comforter," he said, catching hold of it and pulling it over him. "The only reason I decided to share your bed in the first place was to get warm."

She gave him an intimidating glance over her

shoulder before swinging her feet to the floor. Whatever his motive, he needn't have been so blunt about it. "I did wonder," she said irritably.

"Umm. Well, you try spending the night on a davenport that's ten inches too short, and under an air-conditioning vent to boot." He punctuated his remark with a sneeze and tucked the comforter tighter around him. "Are you feeling better?"

It was about time he thought to ask. "Yes, thank you," she said frigidly. "My headache's gone."

"That's good." He punched up the pillow against the headboard behind him and appraised her more carefully. "Unfortunately your black eye isn't."

"Oh, no," she wailed, and headed for the bathroom.

He was right again. She stared at a bedraggled reflection, where part of her forehead and cheek appeared in a Jacob's coat of many colors. Her eye, she noted, specialized in dark blue and yellow. "Damn! Damn! Damn," she muttered, and pushed her fingers through her hair, trying for a semblance of order.

She cast a hesitant look at her folded clothes and a longing one at the shower stall. Since she didn't doubt that Cole would be pounding on the door soon, she stuck her head around the edge of it. "I think I'll . . ." she began, and then broke off when she noticed he was on the bedside phone. An instant later when he'd finished, she tried again. "I thought I'd take a shower and get dressed."

"Okay." He massaged the back of his neck absently. "I just ordered breakfast, so you have ten minutes. You're sure you're up to being vertical that long?"

"Despite appearances, I'm okay," she assured him.

"We'll let the doctor confirm that after breakfast," he said, swinging his legs to the floor. "I suppose if you're going to be formal, I'd better get dressed, too."

"But I'll need to have at least five minutes," she protested.

"Relax. There's another bathroom," he told her over his shoulder.

Stephanie lingered just long enough to confirm that he was still wearing the bottoms of the pajamas she'd noticed earlier, and then she quickly shut the bathroom door before he could shed them.

She hurried through the warm shower and toweled herself dry but she'd barely finished pulling her clothes on when there was an imperative knock and Cole's voice announcing that the eggs were getting cold.

She hastily reached for a comb she'd discovered in the basket of complimentary shampoo and conditioner and dragged it through her hair, deciding not to attempt any cosmetic camouflage until later.

The room-service waiter was just closing the

sitting-room door when she made her way there. Cole was peering beneath the silver covers on the dishes but broke off to pull out a chair for her at the table by the window.

"I am *not* late," she informed him, sitting down in front of a damask place mat. "He was early."

His grin was a rueful acknowledgment. "I wasn't taking any chances. Frankly, I'm starved."

She noticed that he'd shaved and that his hair was still damp from the shower, but his only concession to getting dressed was donning a silk robe the same color as his pajama bottoms.

On intercepting her glance, he pulled the belt tighter and said apologetically, "Sorry, there wasn't time for anything else. Ready for coffee?"

"Yes, please." She pushed her cup over for him to pour. "I was just wondering where all these elegant new clothes came from. The sleep shirt I inherited was lovely."

"Well, there wasn't a chance to get back to the boat, so the lady at the gift shop cooperated. For both of us," he added. "I didn't want to give you an added shock by wandering around in my usual nighttime attire. Or lack of it."

"I see."

"What's the matter? Don't you like poached eggs?"

"They're fine," she said, putting down her fork to break a slice of buttered toast. "Why do you ask?"

"You looked a little strange for a minute," he told her, picking up a piece of bacon and chewing on it. "Probably I should have checked the menu with you."

"It tastes wonderful." There was no doubting the sincerity of her answer but she was still wondering exactly who had put her into the splendid sleep shirt the night before. On the other hand, there was no point in spoiling a perfectly good breakfast with a domestic wrangle.

They ate in silence until Cole had poured a second cup of coffee for both of them. Then he leaned back in his chair and asked, "Now, maybe you'll tell me what you were doing down on the beach yesterday."

His question was so unexpected that Stephanie's swallow of coffee went down the wrong way and there was a recess of a minute or so with Cole patting her on the back while she wiped her streaming eyes and assured him in a thick voice that she was not going to choke to death as well.

When he was convinced, he sat down again and went back to his question like a prizewinning retriever on a field trial. "I thought you were going to stay around the hotel."

"Well, I ran out of things to do, and if I'd loitered in the gift shop longer, they probably would have sent for the house detective. Besides, there isn't any law against strolling on the beach, is there?"

Cole wasn't impressed by her bravado. "Not so far as I know. But you weren't strolling on the beach. At least when you ran into trouble."

Stephanie blotted her lips with the starched white napkin. "I'm not sure what you mean," she said finally.

"Come off it," he scoffed. "I saw you wading in the surf almost ten minutes before I found you stretched out next to the road. What made you change your locale?"

For a moment, she tried to think of an excuse and then decided that it would be foolish not to tell the truth. "I saw you talking to somebody."

His hooded glance wasn't giving anything away. "And?"

"I wondered who it was." She chewed uncertainly on her lip before continuing. "I didn't have the nerve to keep wandering down the beach where you'd see me."

"So you decided to try the high road?"

She nodded. "Something like that. I was just going to peek through the shrubbery and then be on my way. But I wasn't there more than an instant before somebody shoved me from behind. You know the rest." Her hands went out in a graphic gesture. "I never did see who you were with."

His stern mouth twitched in an unwilling grin. "Believe me, he wasn't worth all this."

"He?" The word was out before she realized what a dead giveaway it was.

The grin broadened then. "Why, yes. I didn't

know you had any doubt of that. It was a friend of mine. I'd met him when I was down here on the last trip. Did you think I was trying to recruit another crew member because I had doubts about you?"

"I don't know what I thought." Stephanie couldn't hide her annoyance. "It was obviously a mistake on my part. But apparently I wasn't the only curious person on the beach. Maybe you can explain that."

All the amusement disappeared from Cole's face as he stared across the table at her. "I wish I could. You realize there are two possibilities. Whoever it was could have had designs on you but changed his mind when he heard me coming along the road afterward."

Stephanie gave an involuntary shudder. "I hadn't thought of that. Not really. It seemed more logical that he was doing what I was—"

"Eavesdropping?"

She wrinkled her nose in protest. "It wasn't really that. I wasn't close enough to overhear anything. Of course, I could have interrupted somebody else who was listening . . ." She broke off and then went on with a puzzled expression. "But why would anyone be *that* interested in what you were talking about? Unless it wasn't just an aimless chat on the beach with a friend. You know, now that I think about it, this whole scene seems a little strange. I don't believe I was meant to be the primary target at all."

Cole shoved his chair back with more force

than necessary. "And I think that you're still suffering from that blow on the head," he said, tossing his napkin on the table as he got to his feet. "There are a lot of things to do today, so I'd better get dressed." He started toward the bathroom door, saying over his shoulder, "The doctor will be here to check you out in fifteen minutes."

Stephanie stared after him, too astounded by his abrupt departure to respond. It was strange that he'd cut off their discussion so decisively—stranger still that he had no answer to her accusation that perhaps he was the intended victim.

She was aware that her head had started throbbing again, and she got up from the table to stand on the room's balcony, enjoying the tropical air. Stephanie's lips curved in a wry smile as she thought about it. How strange to think of baked earth smelling good! When she included the breathtaking expanse of ocean in the distance, it was almost too good to be true. If only she could ignore the miserable lump on her forehead!

She sighed then and turned back to the sitting room, relaxing on the sofa where she'd thought Cole was going to spend the night.

It *was* short for him, she decided after putting her legs up and trying to measure. Not horribly short but not great either. She rested her head against the arm cushion and let her eyelids droop as she thought about it.

A brisk knock on the door brought her to life

again a few minutes later. She was just getting to her feet when Cole emerged from the bedroom, looking remarkably well-groomed considering that he'd merely put on khaki-colored shorts and a dark-green T-shirt.

"This should be Doctor Clark," he said, going toward the door. "I'll expect you to abide by his decision. If he says you have to go back to Tortola and rest, that's the final word."

"Oh, but really . . ." Stephanie clamped down on her protest as he opened the door to admit the gray-haired man she'd seen the night before.

Cole nodded and gestured him in the room. "I'll be back when you're finished, Doctor," he told him, carefully keeping his glance from Stephanie as he disappeared into the hallway and closed the door behind him.

Stephanie decided not to say anything about Cole's threat until the doctor had finished her checkup. If the decision turned out to be borderline, she could try for clemency then. There really wasn't much chance to do anything else as the doctor's comment when he opened his bag was, "It's a good thing you're looking better. I'd hate to tangle with him the way he sounds."

"This whole thing has been beyond belief," Stephanie said, extending her arm so that he could take her blood pressure. "Have they had any luck finding out who shoved me?"

He paused before putting the stethoscope to his ears and shook his head. "Not that I've heard.

By now, the whole island has been alerted for any suspicious characters."

His examination was thorough but not prolonged, and Stephanie forgot all about her slight headache when he closed his bag again to announce that there was no reason to change her plans. Provided, he specified, that she took it easy on the boat for the next few days and didn't try any mile-long swims.

"They weren't on my agenda," she told him solemnly, and then chuckled. "Be sure and sound definite when you talk to Cole, will you? I feel like somebody who needs a note to the teacher."

"He did look a bit grim," the doctor agreed, snapping the catch on his bag and preparing to leave. "It's not surprising. He was most concerned about you last night. Almost as if he were responsible for your condition." He paused, waiting for her to refute his words.

Stephanie didn't hesitate to do so. "That's ridiculous. He was a good fifty feet away on the beach when it all happened. Actually, that's about the only thing I'm sure of."

"Well, I wouldn't worry. Mr. Warner will take good care of you from now on." His austere features warmed as he smiled at her from the open doorway. "Actually, he looks as if he's the patient this morning. I'll have to ask how he's feeling. Enjoy your holiday." He gave her a jaunty wave and disappeared into the hall.

Stephanie uttered a relieved sigh and wandered over to see if there were any coffee left in the pot on the table. Cole came back into the room carrying a duffel bag before she had taken more than a couple of swallows.

"I'm okay," she said quickly. "The doctor gave me a clean bill of health."

"I wouldn't go quite that far." His tone was dry. "But he did say that there was no reason for you to give up crewing—especially after he learned that we were only going as far as Virgin Gorda for the next day or so." He strode into the bathroom and came out again, still stuffing what appeared to be his pajamas in the duffel. "Want to put your gear in here, too?" he asked then.

"Yes, please." She got up to head for the bathroom herself. "But all I have to pack is that sleep shirt I wore last night." She turned back to ask, "Does that belong to me?"

He grinned as he checked out the contents of the coffeepot, too. "It certainly does. The lady in the gift shop is an old friend by now. She supplied the pajamas and robe for me too."

"I'm sorry about all the extra bother."

He waved her comment aside. "Don't be. I would have had to break down and buy some before we got very far. And last night you probably would have gone into shock if I'd doled out your pills while I was wrapped in a sheet."

"You're right. I've heard of men in white coats, but one draped in a sheet would have had me out in the hall."

"That's what I was afraid of." He watched her fold her sleep shirt atop his gear and zip the bag closed.

"If you'll tell me what I owe you—" she began then, only to have him brusquely cut her off.

"Don't be absurd." He scowled down at the coffee he'd poured as if wondering why he'd bothered. "You're positive that you want to go on with this trip? I can see you safely back to Tortola this morning and even arrange accommodations on St. John or St. Thomas tonight. You'd probably have a much better time . . ." His voice trailed off as he saw her shake her head. "I'm not sure that you know what you're letting yourself in for," he said then, his tone as grim as his expression.

"You're not doing anything illegal, are you?" Stephanie felt foolish asking the question, but it seemed necessary.

He gave a bark of laughter. "Hardly."

"Well, then . . ." It didn't occur to Stephanie to doubt him. Even more than his words, there was something about the man that convinced her. He could be stern, high-handed, and had already showed that he didn't suffer fools gladly. On the other hand, he had been there all night to make certain that no further harm came to her.

He glanced at her determined face and let out an audible sigh. "Okay. If you're sure." A quick look around and he picked up the duffel bag. "We'll be on our way."

Stephanie nodded, allowing herself a last look around the pleasant room before preceding him into the hall. "Do we have to stop at the desk?" she asked when they reached the lobby.

"No. Everything's been taken care of. We'll go right on down to the dinghy."

Stephanie noticed that this time he didn't hurry down the path toward the landing stage where they had tied the dinghy the night before. She could see it still bobbing on the water before her attention was caught by the interisland ferry at the far end of the pier on its first run of the day. There were several people who had just debarked and were still by the edge of the gangway. The outline of one figure looked familiar and she squinted down the wooden walkway, trying to make sure.

"Isn't that Nevil?" she asked, putting a hand on Cole's forearm to pull him to a stop.

"Nevil Taylor? Where?"

"Down there." She gestured toward the ferry crowd. "He must be checking out another crew this morning—or taking a boat back to Tortola."

"I think you're right." A frown creased Cole's forehead. "It wouldn't hurt to go down and ask him. Want to come along?"

Stephanie wasn't eager to renew her brief acquaintance with the man or explain about the bump on her head. "No, thanks. I'll wait by the dinghy. Want me to hold the duffel?"

He shook his head. "It isn't heavy. I'll be right back."

Stephanie watched him stride down the pier toward the group still lingering by the gangway of the ferry. The sound of laughter floated down toward her on the quiet air and she thought again what a tropical Eden the Virgins were. It was just her bad luck she'd come in contact with the rare unsavory element. A bad apple in paradise, she thought wryly before she walked slowly on down the path to perch on a bollard by the dinghy.

She was relieved when Cole rejoined her a few minutes later.

"You were right," he said, leaning over to toss the duffel in the middle of the dinghy and then dropping down himself. He reached up to grasp her waist and swing her down beside him. "Nevil's due for another checkout cruise this morning. He was surprised to see us still here."

"You didn't tell him—"

Cole shook his head, cutting off her wavery question. "No. There was no reason to. Take care of the painter when I get the motor going, will you?"

She nodded, unreasonably glad that Nevil hadn't come down the pier to extend his greetings in person. Somehow, despite his surface bonhomie, she felt that he hadn't approved of her presence on board.

Her daydreaming came to an abrupt end when

Cole's hand landed on her ankle. "Take care of the line, for Pete's sake," he said, not bothering to hide his impatience.

She realized belatedly that the dinghy motor had come to life and she'd forgotten her part in the proceedings. Scrambling to the bow, she managed to free the line, quickly subsiding into the middle seat again as Cole engaged the clutch and turned the small craft into the open water of the harbor.

Stephanie noted for the first time that several other sloops had come in during the night, almost surrounding the *Bagatelle*. There was one man swimming near the stern of his craft, but he was the only yachtsman on view. She glanced at her watch and saw that it was still early, so perhaps it wasn't surprising that vacationers weren't abovedeck. She thought about remarking on the fact and then decided it wasn't worth shouting over the roar of the outboard. Cole didn't appear inclined for conversation either; he had a relaxed hand on the throttle but the slight frown on his face made her believe that his thoughts weren't on a nose count in the anchorage.

He steered the dinghy alongside the *Bagatelle* shortly afterward and cut the motor when they floated under the boarding ladder. "You go on up," he instructed her. "I'll pass the duffel up to you and take care of things down here."

"Right." She scrambled on deck and took the bag from him an instant later. When he came aboard, she watched him pull up the ladder and secure the painter of the dinghy amidships. Then she escaped down in the cabin so Cole couldn't accuse her of being in the way. She took her sleep shirt out of the duffel and tossed it on her bunk, afterward putting the bag with his belongings in the forward cabin.

"Make sure all the hatches are closed before we get underway," he called as his footsteps could be heard going toward the bow. Evidently he wasn't going to waste any time having extra cups of coffee before getting under way, Stephanie deduced. She hurried to check the hatches as he'd requested.

When she went on deck again, he was standing by the wheel. "Everything shipshape below?" he asked.

She nodded. "I've cleared the galley and all the hatches are closed. What do I do now?"

He was staring at her intently, apparently not liking her wan appearance. "You're sure that you feel up to this?" he asked in brusque tones. "It's going to be a long day and maybe a little rough in spots."

He was clearly hoping that she'd give up and agree to wait for the next ferry back to Tortola. Stephanie wasn't about to cooperate. "I'm perfectly okay," she told him. "I don't have to worry about it being rough. I took a motion-sickness pill just a minute ago."

Cole's eyebrows went up. "In that case, I'll be

lucky if you don't fall asleep before we get out of the harbor."

Stephanie's tone became just as steely as his. "Just tell me what you want me to do." But before he could open his mouth, she hastily qualified her request. "Shall I start the engine now or wait until you've raised the anchor?"

He stared at her a moment longer and finally let out an audible sigh. "Okay, I'll play along, although I think I'm the one who should have had my head examined this morning. Stand by the engine until I get us free and then put it in slow forward. We'll head for the end of the breakwater, but you'll have to thread through the traffic in here on the way."

She nodded, trying to look competent until he started toward the bow again; then she took a shaky breath. Threading through the anchored boats around them wasn't going to be easy. Even yesterday, she'd noticed that the *Bagatelle* had a mind of its own when it came to changing direction. A collision with another yacht would win her a very fast trip back to Tortola indeed. She felt her heartbeat speed up in excitement and then gave a snort of laughter. If Cole thought she was about to fall asleep, he was really mistaken. She'd be more apt to be a basket case when he signaled to start the engine.

Just then she heard the clink of metal against the hull and glanced forward to see him rapidly raising the anchor chain.

"Start the engine," he called back to her. "Neutral."

Her thumb went out for the black button even as she echoed his command, "Neutral it is."

The throaty roar of the motor showed there was nothing wrong there, and Stephanie, for a split second, didn't know whether to be pleased or disappointed. She didn't have time to dwell on it as she saw Cole heaving the anchor aboard.

"Slow forward," he called over his shoulder.

Stephanie nodded and gingerly changed the throttle as the schooner moved in the current. She grasped the wheel as if it were a lifeline, and turned toward the end of the breakwater.

The first twenty feet were all right, and then she noticed the two anchored yachts swinging directly in her path. Should she turn right or left? "Which way do I go?" she shrieked at Cole, who was still coiling the anchor line in the bow.

He bobbed up like a Mylar balloon, taking in the scene immediately. "Port." His stentorian command cut through the air and he gestured in that direction, so she had no doubts.

As she automatically spun the wheel in response, she became aware that, by then, every yacht in the harbor either had anxious people on deck or wary heads at portholes. Evidently her call for help and Cole's stern reply had triggered unscheduled lifeboat drills on every craft within hailing distance.

Stephanie mentioned it to Cole when he reached the stern an instant later and took over the steering duties. "Did you see the terror on that woman's face?"

He turned back, frowning. "Where?"

"That last schooner—when I passed their bow."

His shoulders shook with laughter. "We weren't that close."

Stephanie shivered, remembering. "Close enough. The tom-toms are probably already beating to warn Virgin Gorda we're coming."

"You're imagining things." Cole spoke absently, more intent on getting around the end of the breakwater and heading them toward the island of Virgin Gorda when they reached open water. "Besides, you'll be more experienced by the time we reach our moorage at The Bitter End tonight."

"Are you being funny?"

He stared at her. "What do you mean?"

"Is there really a place called The Bitter End?"

"There really is. You'll find it on the northeast coast of Virgin Gorda if you check out the chart. Hold on." He stopped her when she started toward the cabin. "I need you to take the wheel first while I get the sails up. There's no point in using the motor from now on." As she approached the wheel warily, he said, "It's okay. There's open water all around you. Just keep on this course." His eyes narrowed as he surveyed her. "You can manage that, can't you?"

His tone was so condescending that Stephanie wanted to haul off and hit him—anything to disturb the monumental self-assurance that radiated from every line of his tall frame. He must have known how she felt because his expression almost dared her to, and that was what made her hedge her bets. It was as if he were just looking for a reason to put her ashore, for he hadn't been able to convince her earlier with reasonable argument.

Stephanie moved around to hang on to the wheel. "Isn't it nice? The motion isn't bothering me at all today." She added the last in a tone that was intended to raise his blood pressure twenty points.

Apparently she succeeded, because he hesitated just an instant longer to say, "Wonderful," in a way that meant nothing of the kind, before going toward the bow.

She stood at the wheel watching him while keeping a careful eye on their course. He changed the dinghy to bob at their stern and then raised the mainsail and jib. She was careful not to show any apprehension over the way the *Bagatelle* was heeling when he came back to the stern again.

He leaned down and killed the engine before saying, "I'll take over now. If you want to be useful, I could do with a cup of coffee."

She merely nodded and asked, "Anything to go with it?"

"I think there are some crackers in that locker by the stove."

"Right. I won't be long."

She managed to get down the steps safely, although the *Bagatelle* was showing more motion than the previous day. Thank heaven for motion pills, she thought, but she didn't waste any time thinking about the stuffy air in the cabin as she filled the kettle and turned on a burner at the gas stove. While the water was heating, she took time to put away the sleep shirt in the tiny locker by her bed and then unearthed her cotton brimmed hat. She managed to pull it on at an angle avoiding the bruised side of her forehead. At least the brim would ensure that she didn't get a pink nose to add to her color spectrum.

By then, the water was boiling and she poured it into two mugs before adding instant coffee. Afterward, she stowed the kettle in the sink and found the box of cheese crackers Cole had mentioned. Carefully, she went up the stairs with his coffee and the box.

"Aren't you having anything?" he asked after taking them.

"On the next trip," she assured him. "Want anything else?"

"Not right now, thanks." He stowed the crackers on the deck and took a sip of coffee before putting the mug by the binnacle.

There wasn't any more conversation after that for a while and Stephanie relaxed as she realized the silence wasn't an unpleasant one.

It was only after they'd finished the coffee and she'd rinsed the dirty mugs that Cole said,

"If you want to take a rest, this will be a good time. It'll be a while before we get to where we're going. Just take the wheel while I trim the sails and then you'll be off duty until lunch."

Stephanie quickly took over and watched him easily move along the slanted deck as if he'd spent every day at sea. It wasn't until he came back and took over the steering duties a little later that she asked hesitantly, "Is it okay if I just lounge around up here?"

"For Lord's sake, I didn't expect you to sit in the dinghy," he said, not bothering to hide his impatience. "You're part of the crew—not a galley slave." Then, seeing the stony polite expression that came over her face, he shook his head. "I'm sorry. Do whatever you want, of course. But if you're going to stay up here, at least get some cushions out of that locker. And I'd appreciate your finding my sunglasses—they should be somewhere in my cabin."

"Okay." She smiled with relief and headed for the stairs again. Cole's apology had helped immensely, although she had no doubt that he was still unhappy about her presence on board. The fact that he had used her so sparingly showed that he knew she wasn't great in the crew line. It was going to be hard to convince him that she was a whiz in the galley when peanut-butter sandwiches were evidently topping the menu for lunch.

At least she could make coffee and fetch sunglasses, she told herself. The latter wasn't difficult, since they were resting right next to the duffel bag on his bunk. She thought about unpacking the bag and then decided against it. The way things were, she was balancing on a very thin line. One wrong remark and she'd be shipped out. Virgin Gorda would serve for that just as well as Peter Island, which was growing smaller behind the *Bagatelle*'s stern. Cole was too civilized to believe in modern-day keelhauling with an unsatisfactory crew, and Stephanie was damned if she'd give him a chance to find an alternative.

Chapter 5

It was a pleasant day, despite Stephanie's misgivings. As she thought when she was constructing the peanut-butter sandwiches for lunch, it would be a poor person who couldn't enjoy a day of bright sunshine, sapphire-blue water, and a nudging breeze just forceful enough to keep the *Bagatelle*'s sails full.

About noon, when she and Cole were munching on their sandwiches, he gestured toward the island of Virgin Gorda, which they were skirting on the starboard side. "The Baths," he said, indicating an area with an unusual rock formation in the middle of the beach. "One of the better swimming holes in this part of the country."

"At least a popular one," Stephanie commented, "judging from the number of boats anchored offshore. What's so unusual about the place?"

Cole shrugged and swallowed another bite of his sandwich before replying. "There's a lot of nice sand—a gradual drop-off so people can bring their kids—all the usual. And, no, we can't stop to sample the amenities today."

"I didn't say anything about stopping."

He seemed amused at her instant defense. "Maybe not, but you looked like Poor Pitiful Pearl when I described the beach. Perhaps you'll have better luck when we get to The Bitter End. If this wind keeps up, we should be able to tie up in late afternoon."

"I hadn't realized you were on such a strict schedule," Stephanie said, giving the Baths area another quick look before focusing her attention on Cole as he relaxed at the wheel.

"It wasn't in the original plan," he admitted after a pause. "Now it seems like the best thing to do."

Stephanie wondered if she dared ask exactly why it was the best thing to do, and decided against it.

There was a silence that wasn't so comfortable for the next minute or two after that. Then Cole rubbed his jaw and cast her an irritable look. "Actually," he said, stressing all four syllables of the word, "I've made plans to meet somebody tonight at The Bitter End. A friend of mine. Somebody I met on my last trip."

Stephanie's heart seemed to flip-flop at his words, but she kept her expression noncommittal. "I see. Maybe you'd prefer that I stayed aboard."

"You have to eat." His tone was still impatient. "Perhaps you won't mind if I bring you back here early after dinner. It wouldn't hurt for you to get some extra rest, considering all that happened last night."

"You're probably right." She kept her voice matter-of-fact. "I'll be happy to do whatever's convenient for you. Want anything else to eat? There's a box of cookies down in the cabin that I forgot to bring up."

"That sounds good." Cole looked relieved at the change of subject and handed an empty soda can to her when she stood up and turned toward the stairs. "Dump this in the garbage bag, will you; and bring me a fresh one."

"Of course." Stephanie took it from him, careful to keep a pleasant expression all the way to the cabin. Only when she reached the bottom of the stairs did she bite down on the edge of her lower lip and fling the can into the plastic garbage bag so hard that it almost ricocheted against the cabinet door. Damn that man! He was just like every other attractive male! Probably there'd be a woman waiting at the dock each time they anchored from now on. Maybe there was even a disappointed female at Peter Island who'd been stood up for the evening because his last-minute crew member came a cropper with a palm tree.

Stephanie stomped into the compact head that was allotted for her use and sloshed cold water over her face—trying to cool both her temperature and her anger. One thing for sure: she wouldn't let Cole know how his social schedule had affected her. She caught a glimpse of her features in the mirror above the basin as she reached for a towel, and scowled back at her reflection. She couldn't blame the man for trying other turf, since she still looked like the loser in a tag-team wrestling match. It was a wonder that he was willing to have dinner with her in public. Maybe he was afraid she'd sue him for abuse if three meals a day weren't forthcoming, she thought as she patted her face dry with the towel.

"Hey . . . Are you okay down there?"

Cole's shout brought her head up in a hurry and she composed her expression before appearing at the bottom of the stairs.

"I'm fine. Did you want anything?"

"Just something cold to drink. This is thirsty work." He bestowed an indulgent smile to show that he wasn't blaming her for the fact that she couldn't handle the only request he'd made since lunch.

"Oh, Lord!" Stephanie could have groaned aloud but whirled around to look for the soda so fast that her head started pounding again. "I'll get it right away."

After that, it was more of the same. Cole would occasionally ask her to take the wheel when he wanted to trim the sails. Each time he was careful to indicate their course, telling her in quiet, measured tones.

In late afternoon she watched him lower the

jib as they approached the northeast coast of Virgin Gorda. She quickly moved away from the wheel when he came back to the stern to take over again.

"It shouldn't be long now before we can tie up for the night," he announced as he changed their course to starboard to approach the channel for Gorda Sound. "That's Necker Island out there to port," he went on conversationally. "Sometimes it's hard to distinguish one from another down here, since the vegetation looks about the same."

A sudden gust of wind made him frown and cast an appraising glance at the mainsail.

"Can I do anything?" Stephanie asked quickly.

"Probably it wouldn't hurt to go in under power," he said, sounding as if he were thinking aloud. Then he turned to her and said, "Take over the wheel for a bit while I lower the main. And for God's sake, watch the channel markers. There are coral heads all over the place and they're definitely to be avoided. I won't be long," he assured her after he watched her for a few seconds to make sure that she wasn't about to try a U-turn in midchannel as soon as he turned his back.

Stephanie let out a breath of relief when the big sail came down and the boat steadied in the currents. "Start the engine," Cole called a moment later from where he was rolling the mainsail. "Keep your eyes on those channel markers. You're doing fine." The last showed he was pleasantly surprised.

"Bully for me," Stephanie muttered under her breath, but she couldn't help a slight smile as she leaned over to touch the button for the engine.

They came into civilization with a vengeance some fifteen minutes later when they passed Saba Rock and the luxurious resort called The Bitter End loomed up on the port side of Gorda Sound.

The steep-roofed housing units were scattered among the greenery on the gentle hillside, looking like something out of a South Seas painting. She could see that most of the villas had open porches so their occupants could fully enjoy the sweeping vistas of busy Gorda Sound.

The harbor in front of the resort was cluttered with all sizes of craft from Windsurfers zipping through the mooring buoys to a palatial yacht anchored at the far end. There was a white sand beach near one of the bigger buildings. It, too, was crowded.

"Okay," Cole said after a searching look around the harbor. "It's time for you to go to work again. I want you to take the wheel while I try to latch on to one of those mooring buoys. Thank God there are still a few available. I'm glad we didn't arrive any later."

Stephanie rubbed the side of her face nervously as she surveyed the small red balls bobbing in the water. "Exactly how do you latch on to one?" she asked, taking over the wheel as he started forward.

"With a boat hook. Follow my hand signals and cut the throttle when we approach."

He didn't waste any more time and, a minute later, stood straight at the bow with a metal hook in his hand. "Aim for the one in front of the sloop with the red sails," he called back. "Approach it on the port side and go into neutral when I tell you."

Stephanie hung on to the wheel so tightly that her knuckles were white as she maneuvered the *Bagatelle* past the sloop Cole had mentioned, and she quickly responded when he shouted, "Neutral." A moment later, he was on his stomach along the deck with his head and shoulders over the rail. Stephanie stood on tiptoe while still hanging on to the wheel, trying to steer the right course. Two or three seconds later, she saw the red ball float by the stern after Cole had made an unsuccessful pass at the line under it with his boat hook.

"Go around again," he called, pushing up on an elbow. "Cut your speed earlier next time. We want to be almost dead in the water when we get abeam of it."

"I'll do my best," Stephanie yelled back, and pushed the throttle forward slightly as she started to turn the *Bagatelle* for another attempt. She threaded carefully through the anchored boats in the harbor and made a mental resolve never to complain about parallel-parking a car again. At least cars had brakes and she'd learned that the sloop had a mind of its own when it came to stopping.

"Better cut your speed." Cole's warning brought her back to the present in a hurry as she realized that the *Bagatelle* was on course for another try at the buoy. She reached hurriedly to pull the throttle back into neutral and chewed nervously on her lower lip as they approached the red ball.

Then there was a sudden movement at the bow as Cole brought the boat hook into play. "Got it," he called triumphantly. "Cut the engine."

Stephanie's dive for the button was almost as fast as his maneuver, but she still found time to stare in fascination as he made the sloop fast. She was frowning down at the swift currents going past the hull when he made his way back a few minutes later.

"What's the matter? You look worried," he commented, absently wiping his perspiring forehead with the back of his hand.

Stephanie gestured toward their buoy. "How do you know that it will hold?" Her glance around the crowded harbor was evidence of her concern. "This is hardly the place for getting away from it all. It's like a national-park campground on the Fourth of July."

Cole nodded ruefully. "I know, and it's not even the height of the season. But you don't have to worry about the buoys. They're anchored on the bottom and I've cleated the line securely. However, it doesn't hurt to make sure. I'll dive down and make sure that everything's okay."

Stephanie looked longingly at the clear water lapping against the stern, but Cole spoke over his shoulder before she could say anything.

"I wouldn't recommend your going in," he advised as he started down to the cabin. "At least not here. There's a good shallow beach by the club that's more your speed."

Stephanie was still fuming at that remark when he came on deck a little later, his tanned length looking even more formidable than usual in the brief swim trunks that hugged his hips.

"What did you mean, more my speed?" she asked, trying to keep her glance safely at shoulder height. "I'm a pretty good swimmer."

"That has nothing to do with it," he said, searching through a side locker and finally coming up with a scuba mask. "After that blow on your head last night, you're supposed to be taking it easy. That doesn't mean swimming laps in Gorda Sound." He put the rope ladder over the side and prepared to go down. "You hold the fort, this shouldn't take long. And if you want to do something practical, get ready for dinner. I called in a reservation on the radio a few minutes ago and we'll have to be on time."

He adjusted the scuba mask to his satisfaction and stepped down into the water, disappearing beneath the surface with hardly a ripple.

Stephanie ignored his instructions, making her way to the bow instead, observing when he surfaced by the buoy to inspect the sturdy line that was keeping the *Bagatelle* attached to it. She hoped it was secure because the sloop was moving restlessly in the strong currents like a Thoroughbred waiting for the starting gates to open. She watched Cole submerge again, this time obviously to check the buoy anchor on the bottom. She lingered only long enough to view his head surfacing again before she relaxed and started for her cabin. By then, the peanut-butter sandwich she'd had for lunch was only a memory, so she had no intention of missing dinner.

Only a little later she heard the boarding ladder being replaced on deck and Cole coming down the stairs.

"Is everything all right?" she asked, poking her head around the door of her tiny cabin.

"As ordered," he said casually, not stopping on the way toward his own cabin. He was using a towel to blot some of the water from his shoulders, but he was still leaving a trail on the wooden floor.

Stephanie wanted to ask him what women wore for dinner ashore at Gorda Sound, but from the look on his face she decided this wasn't the time for it.

As a result, her own expression was hard to read when she went on deck fifteen minutes later. She was wearing a fuchsia cotton jumpsuit of crinkly cotton with a boat neckline, ruffled sleeves, and pants that reached midcalf. The fact that it flattered her tanned skin and was ultra-feminine as well as practical had been responsible for her decision.

She watched Cole's eyebrows go up, and for an instant there was something in his glance that made her draw in her breath before he said, "I'll have to make sure that you don't catch a wave in the dinghy. It would be a shame to spoil the effects of all that."

Stephanie relaxed slightly. "It's washable, so it really doesn't matter." Her gaze slid over his own casual attire of beige polished cotton slacks and a short-sleeved navy sport shirt. His hair was still damp, but he looked trim and comfortable. "What time is our dinner reservation?" she asked, trying to sound nonchalant.

"About forty minutes from now," he said, glancing at his watch. "I thought if we took off right away, you'd have a chance for a drink or a look through the shops." As her expression brightened, he added, "I was sure that might strike a responsive chord. Neither rain, nor sleet, nor a bump on the head can keep a woman from the sound of a busy cash register."

"The postal service could sue you for slander," Stephanie told him severely as she took a tighter grip on her purse. "I'm ready right now. Do we have to lock up or anything?" she asked looking toward the cabin.

"Boat people are a pretty honest bunch," Cole said, gesturing her amidships, where he'd tied the dinghy in readiness. "If you have any crown jewels, you might want to bring them along."

"I left them behind this trip, so I don't have to worry." She followed him on the deck, glad of her rubber-soled espadrilles when they reached the boarding ladder. "Shall I go first?"

"Better let me," he said, swinging easily over the railing and down into the center of the bobbing dinghy. "Take it easy," he said, keeping a firm grip on her waist as she clambered down. "Sit down here in the middle. The bow is apt to catch some spray." Then, while she was still settling onto the seat, he'd loosened the painter and was back working on the outboard.

It started at the first pull. Stephanie swallowed an inclination to giggle as she thought that it wouldn't have dared do anything else. And then, a moment later, she clutched her purse between her knees and hung on to the sides of the pitching dinghy as they cut across the currents and the wake of an incoming cruiser to head for the resort dock some five hundred feet away.

She was happy for the wide legs of the jumpsuit when they reached the pier steps a little later.

"Get out here," Cole instructed. "I'll tie up down the way a bit, but it'll be easier for you if there are stairs."

"You're right about that," she told him ruefully, standing up and keeping a firm grip on the side of the steps. "Otherwise I do a wonderful impression of a beached porpoise."

He grinned in response. "I'll have to see that sometime. Right now, that outfit of yours deserves better." Then, when she'd reached the pier, he said, "Go on down to where the action is. I'll catch up with you."

"How about the gift shop?"

"How about it?" The grin materialized again for an instant before he revved the throttle on the outboard and headed out for another pier where dinghys were tying up.

For an instant, the wooden planks underneath her feet seemed to match the heaving deck of the *Bagatelle*, but Stephanie took a determined breath and marched down toward the resort buildings clustered at the base of the hillside.

She stopped when she reached the main walkway, which was thronged with vacationers, most of them informally dressed in shorts and swimsuits but some in more formal gear who were obviously headed for the big bar and restaurant to her left.

Ahead of her was the gift shop, where she'd promised to meet Cole, but discreet signs also indicated a grocery, sport shop, and numbers of the vacation villas to the right. She decided to wander down that way and see what was going on. There was a boat-rental section first, bordered by an open area that showed there were also Windsurfers to be had if the boater wanted company. Apparently many of the holiday guests made their way by plane to Gorda Sound and then took to the water in rental craft.

Her curiosity satisfied, Stephanie was on the point of going back when a man who was talking to a deeply tanned individual in swim trunks nearby caught her glance. He'd changed from his scruffy tank top of the day before, but there was no doubting that it was their checkout skipper, Nevil Taylor. For an instant, Stephanie debated going over to say hello, and then she turned quickly away. She really hadn't liked him in the first place and it was more than likely he'd think a chance meeting could be an excuse for sharing their table for dinner.

She walked quickly back to the gift-shop entrance after that, debating whether or not to tell Cole about her discovery.

When she saw him at the end of the pier near the gift shop talking to a tall, fair-haired man with a beaky nose and sunburned skin, her steps slowed and then stopped. Probably the diplomatic thing would be to detour into the gift shop and leave Cole undisturbed.

Unfortunately he glanced around and saw her before she could put her plan into action. Annoyance momentarily showed on his face, although, an instant later, his features smoothed to their usual imperturbable mien.

"Stephanie, sorry I've held you up," he said, beckoning her to his side. "Come and meet a friend of mine. May I present Ian MacLean—one of the natives here. Ian, Stephanie Church, who's crewing for me on the *Bagatelle*."

"How do you do, Miss Church." MacLean's accent was standard British rather than the distinctive tempo of the Virgins. "You picked some good weather for your holiday, but then Cole always seems to come out on the winning side. In most everything."

His frankly admiring smile showed that he wasn't just talking about the climate, and Stephanie smiled back automatically. He was probably closer to forty than thirty, but his courtly manners oozed charm.

The same couldn't be said of Cole. He had a preoccupied expression that showed he wasn't in the mood for issuing compliments. It was so different from the way he'd acted in the dinghy that Stephanie gave him an uncertain look and then made up her mind.

"I'm sure you two have things to talk about," she said, keeping her tone light. "Have I time to look around the gift shop or maybe you'd like to change our dinner arrangements—"

"You don't have to be diplomatic," Cole said, his voice dry. "I've already asked Ian to join us, but he turned me down."

"Nothing personal," the Britisher said hastily. "I just had made other plans and I can't cancel them. Not a good idea at this point," he added, turning back to Cole. "Perhaps tomorrow—if you're spending the day on Gorda Sound."

"I'll get in touch and let you know what our schedule is," Cole told him. "We'll probably be going over to Prickly Pear in the forenoon. The waters there are especially good for scuba," he added for Stephanie's benefit.

"Well, maybe I'll see you then." Ian gave them both a brief salute before turning to stride down the path that Stephanie had explored earlier.

Cole glanced at his watch and put his hand on Stephanie's waist, steering her toward the bar and dining area. "We might as well go in and have a drink at our table if it's ready."

From his demeanor, he could have been announcing an impending visit to the dentist, and any hopes Stephanie might have had for getting to know each other better over dinner *à deux* dimmed. Feminine pride tempted her to tell him that they really didn't have to have dinner together, and then she thought of the barren galley aboard the *Bagatelle*. She was willing to settle on corn flakes for breakfast, but damned if she was going to exist on another peanut-butter sandwich for dinner!

"Something long and cool sounds wonderful," she said, trying to sound as if that was the only thought she had in mind. "I don't think we're very original, though. This place is jammed."

"I know." That unruffled expression had settled over Cole's features again. "I'll check with the maître d'," he said, steering her through the crowded tables of the bar to the entrance of the even more dimly lit dining area.

Stephanie remained a few feet away when he talked to the man, who was barricaded behind a pile of menus. She was too far away to see if any money changed hands, but a moment later Cole beckoned and they were following a trim hostess through tables filled with noisy diners.

She barely had time to notice the expanse of dark wood and rafters decorated with South Seas decor. Flickering candles in hurricane lamps were on each table to provide most of the illumination.

Stephanie looked over to Cole when they were seated and surveying menus a minute or so later. "You didn't bring a flashlight, did you?"

He looked up, startled. "No. Why?"

She gestured around them. "This is either for atmosphere or they don't want us to see what we're eating. That could mean a catastrophe in the kitchen."

"Maybe they're trimming the electricity budget," Cole said. "Although I doubt if they have to worry about that." He closed his menu with a decisive gesture. "I could see enough to find a New York steak. How does that sound to you?"

"Heavenly." Stephanie put her menu on the table in front of her and leaned back in her chair, determined to start enjoying the evening out.

There was a little more discussion when the waiter arrived, but it wasn't long afterward before she was sipping a frosty glass of tonic water and Cole took an appreciative swallow of his ale.

"Ian MacLean seemed very pleasant," she said, wondering if she could find out what she wanted to know under the guise of casual conversation.

"Uh-huh." Cole's attention seemed to be riveted on the next table, where one of the dining-room captains was industriously concocting a Caesar-salad dressing.

"Was your last trip down here the first time you'd met?" Stephanie's voice rose slightly despite her resolve to keep calm.

Cole brought his attention back to her, but he wasn't enthusiastic about it. "The first time for what?"

"I was trying to find out when you met Ian MacLean." Her words came out like the ice cubes she was swirling in her glass.

"Oh, a year or so ago." Cole stared at his ale and took another swallow.

"Here?"

His sigh could be heard even across the table. "No. Actually it was in Savannah, when I was down there visiting my mother's relatives." His eyebrows drew together. "Did I say something funny?"

"No, not really," Stephanie replied, although her lips still curved in a smile. "It was just that mention of Savannah."

"Go on. There must be a punch line."

"Not really. It reminded me of a woman I met when I visited there. A real Georgian through and through. She said that in Atlanta, people ask you where you work. In Macon, they ask your religion. In Augusta, they ask your grandmother's maiden name. And in Savannah . . ." Her voice trailed off tantalizingly.

She had all his attention then. "And in Savannah," he prompted.

"In Savannah, they just ask what you'd like to drink."

He burst out laughing and was still chuckling when the waiter arrived with their salad. "That must have been why my grandfather decided to settle there," he said when they were alone again.

"But you don't live there now?" she probed delicately.

"Nope." He sounded amused. "My folks turned me into a 'damned Yankee' at an early age, but the southern branch of the family ignores it when I go calling. Geography is never mentioned."

"Sort of like a dreaded disease."

He was intent on cutting a tomato slice into a more manageable bite. "Or a terminal illness. Why all this interest in my family tree?"

Stephanie felt her cheeks redden under his amused scrutiny. "You must have heard about women vacationing alone. We travel with a Dun and Bradstreet directory and a volume of *Who's Who* in our luggage."

"I'm afraid you'll come up with a blank page when you get down to W in the alphabet."

"That's all right." She managed to match his tone. "I left in such a hurry this trip that I forgot to bring them along, so you don't have to worry."

"What a relief." Then he reverted to his older-brother role—the kind she'd been seeing all day. "I'd suggest wine to go with your dinner, but you'd better wait until another day when we know your head's back to normal."

Not "would you like" or "what do you think,"

but merely "you'd better wait." As a labor-mediation consultant, he'd be a total disaster, Stephanie thought. On the other hand, the joint chiefs of staff were missing a real bet for a new recruit.

It wasn't until they were on cups of coffee and waiting for their bill that it occurred to her that Cole hadn't enlarged on his comment about Ian MacLean. "About your friend, Mr. MacLean," she said. "Is he taking a vacation, too?"

"Ian's lived on Tortola for some time," he responded finally.

She couldn't be certain, but Cole appeared to be relieved that their waiter presented their check at that moment and disrupted any further conversation. After all the business had been taken care of, Cole got to his feet and said, "I'd better be getting you back to the *Bagatelle*."

"Whatever you say." She stood up and reached for her purse.

"I'm sorry that you won't have time for a quick tour of the gift shop," he said, urging her ahead of him through the crowded dining-room tables toward the entrance. "Perhaps another time."

Stephanie was darned if she'd display any evidence of hurt feelings at his obvious desire to plonk her aboard the sloop so he could carry on with his social life ashore. When they reached the main pier, Cole offered to walk around and get the dinghy, bringing it to where he'd let her off before. "That's silly," she said. "I'm certainly able to go with you. Besides, I'd like to take a closer look where they rent the boats."

"Isn't the *Bagatelle* big enough for you or did you plan on a busman's holiday tomorrow?" Cole asked whimsically as they walked along toward the shorter pier.

She kept her voice demure. "I thought I'd check out some alternatives in case you decide to go it alone."

"And how do you plan to do that out here?" he asked, clearly amused. "There might be more action if you'd stayed in the bar."

She pretended to pull up. "Now he tells me."

Cole put a firm hand in the middle of her back to urge her along. "Another time perhaps. Definitely not now."

"Ah, well." She managed a disappointed sigh. "Then I'll just have to see if Nevil's still around."

This time it was Cole who pulled up, paying no attention to the obvious honeymoon couple behind them. He let them go around and then caught Stephanie's forearm in an iron grip. "Say that again."

She pulled free without much effort but couldn't resist saying, "I have enough bruises already, thanks." Then, when she saw his frown, she added quickly, "I merely wondered if Nevil was still around the boatyard."

"Nevil Taylor, our checkout skipper?"

She nodded, puzzled at his interest. "That's right. I thought I saw him when I was wandering around here before dinner. He was talking to somebody down by that office. At least, I'm almost sure it was Nevil. I didn't want to go any closer because I wasn't eager to renew our acquaintance."

"I can understand that." Cole rubbed the side of his nose absently, then started walking again toward where he'd tied the dinghy. "I suppose I shouldn't be surprised if he is in the neighborhood. Checkout skippers work the whole island chain."

"Do you want to look around for him?"

He didn't slacken his pace. "I can't think of any reason to. As a matter of fact, I don't imagine he'd be keen to see us, either."

"He thought you were all right, but I could tell that I didn't make the grade. He didn't come right out and say it, but I had the feeling that he only recognizes two places for women."

"You mean the galley and—"

"Exactly." She cut in before Cole could finish his sentence. Then, intent on changing the subject as they came alongside the dinghy, she added, "If I'm to keep my dignity, you'll have to get in first. In this outfit, scooting on my derriere—"

"—wouldn't enhance your social standing," Cole agreed.

"Plus picking up some splinters on the way," Stephanie decided with another look at the wooden pier.

Fortunately she didn't have to worry about it because Cole swung himself down into the dinghy and, reaching up, easily plucked her off and into the boat. "Can you take care of the painter when I get this thing going?" he asked, settling into the stern alongside the motor.

Stephanie nodded and did as he asked on the first muted roar of the outboard. She hastily subsided on the seat again, landing a little heavier that she'd planned when they caught the wake of an incoming craft. Cole chose to overlook it, seemingly intent on threading them out into the less crowded water of the harbor.

By then, there were so many craft at anchor that Stephanie wondered how he'd ever locate the *Bagatelle* in darkness when he decided to abandon his nightlife ashore. She brushed off a spray of water irritably, thinking it would serve him right if he wandered around Gorda Sound half the night. Although from the admiring glances he'd received in the dining room from the women at an adjoining table, he'd probably be welcomed with enthusiasm if he tied up to the wrong sloop.

"Is your head bothering you again?" Cole raised his voice to be heard over the growl of the outboard.

Startled, she looked back and then said, "No. It's okay. Why?"

"You looked as if something was bothering you. You shouldn't be alone on board if you're under the weather. There might be a vacant villa in the resort if you'd rather stay ashore."

Stephanie's pulse rate, which had started thumping at his first comment, settled back in its usual rut. Even staying alone on the *Bagatelle* for part of the night was better than being shunted off to a villa on the hillside in splendid isolation.

"I'm perfectly okay," she told him in a manner that didn't invite any more discussion of the subject. As he throttled down when they rounded the *Bagatelle*'s stern and came alongside, she reached up and steadied them at the boarding ladder.

Surprisingly, Cole followed her aboard but only to pick up his jacket and switch on the sloop's anchor light at the panel in the cabin. Then he turned to Stephanie and gave her another long, searching look. "You should be okay while I'm gone. If anything bothers you, get on the radiotelephone here. Just call the resort and tell them what's wrong. Okay?"

She nodded, wanting to ask him how long he'd be but deciding against it. "I'll see you later or in the morning, then. Shall I leave a light in the porthole?" she asked flippantly when he started for the dinghy.

"I wouldn't," he said, giving her a wry look over his shoulder. "It might give you more company than you planned on. Just read a good book and try for an early night."

It was difficult for her to maintain a pleasant expression after that. Somehow Stephanie managed until she had waved the dinghy on its way and then went to plunk herself down by the wheel. At any other time she would have enjoyed the freedom of the sloop as it rode at anchor in one of the most romantic locations in the western hemisphere. All around the harbor were forty- and fifty-foot luxury craft with their owners still on deck to enjoy the last bit of daylight. There was a barbecue grill attached to the stern of one nearby sloop and every once in a while a mouth-watering smell would waft its way toward the *Bagatelle*. And every boat had at least two people aboard, Stephanie noted. One of each sex, she confirmed, which made her more disgruntled than ever.

Since she wasn't hungry and she didn't have anyone to talk to, that only left the scenery, but even that wouldn't last much longer as the sun disappeared.

At the same time, the breeze freshened and Stephanie rubbed her arms absently, deciding that cotton ruffles on the sleeves might be pretty but didn't do much for warmth. Probably the smartest thing to do would be try the cabin and look for a good book.

As she descended the stairs, the temperature seemed to rise by fifteen degrees. It wasn't surprising, she discovered, since she'd forgotten to open the hatches and allow for decent ventilation below deck.

Even after fixing that, she decided that it would be more comfortable to sit around in a pair of shortie pajamas and enjoy the little cool air that was circulating. Fortunately she had a pair of cotton broadcloth ones on the top of her belongings. She undressed quickly, stopping only to turn on the minuscule fan that was supposed to cool the stern cabin.

The tiny fan tried valiantly to do the job but the whine of its motor sounded like an amplified mosquito. Stephanie perched on the edge of her mattress and scowled at it for an instant before deciding that she'd read out in the galley, where to space wasn't so limited.

She switched off the fan and moved out into the eating space after picking up a paperback novel.

It should have been fine except that the cabin was too hot, the reading light too dim, and the motion of the sloop too pronounced.

"Dammit all to hell!" she announced to the empty cabin after she'd tried to ignore all three for a half-hour. A quick look up the stairs showed that darkness had descended so that there wasn't any reason she couldn't go on deck without putting on a robe.

It was almost pitch-black as she reached the top of the stairs, but the slight breeze felt wonderful after the stuffy air below and somehow the motion of the sloop didn't seem at all objectionable when there was a salt tang connected with it. She took a deep breath and then went back toward the wheel to switch on the tiny hooded binnacle light. It provided just enough illumination for comfort and she sat down alongside on a vinyl cushion, happy that things seemed to be looking up.

The other yachts just showed anchor lights

and glimmers from behind closed curtains on the portholes, but there was still plenty of light from the buildings on shore. The resort apparently was full of holidaymakers intent on not wasting a minute of their leisure time. Occasionally the sound of music and shriekes of laughter wafted across the water. Stephanie thought about Cole in the midst of the festivities and muttered an unladylike phrase under her breath.

Which was absurd, she told herself, and leaned back on her cushion, determined to enjoy the rhythmic motion of the *Bagatelle* and the fresh ocean air. Some time later, she jerked erect, surprised that she'd apparently dozed off in the quiet of the evening, propped against the side of the sloop. It wouldn't do to be sitting there any longer, she decided, since she didn't want Cole to think that she'd been waiting around for his return. Better to go below and hope that the cabin was a little cooler so that she could sleep in comfort on a mattress.

By the time she'd brushed her teeth and washed her face, the prospect of bed sounded even more attractive. She closed the door of her compartment, arranged her pillow, decided against turning on the noisy fan, and closed her eyes.

Fifteen minutes later, she sat up groaning and reached across to turn on both the dim overhead light and the fan. Her next move was to unbutton her pajama top down to her navel and punch her hot pillow into position behind her so that she could try reading. She'd barely opened her book when the sound of an outboard motor approaching made her hastily flip off both the fan and the light before shoving the book under her pillow. She remained immobile when she heard the motor cut out abruptly and, a minute or so later, the sound of footsteps on deck. It was only then that it occurred to her that it might be someone other than Cole. Not that she could do anything about it, she concluded as barely perceptible noises could be heard on the stairs.

A moment later, she let out her breath in relief as the cabin light by the galley was switched on after she heard the clatter of the metal tea kettle as it was shoved inadvertently into the sink. There was also a muffled, profane phrase to accompany it.

Stephanie clamped her lips together to keep from giggling aloud as she heard Cole go forward to his cabin and then come back again to turn out the galley light. When his cabin door closed an instant later, she let out a sigh and pushed up on her elbow. So much for her hopes that he'd check to see if she were still among the living!

She turned on her cabin light again since she was so wide awake that sleep was out of the question. A half-hour later, when all was quiet except for the creaking of the hull, Stephanie decided that she was going to drown in her own perspiration. By then, her earlier conclusion that the bulkhead behind her pillow was directly over the *Bagatelle*'s engine proved to be true. Apparently the heat from the day's run had been captured below decks and was now seeping upward. Even the silly little fan couldn't alleviate that, and its noise would probably keep Cole awake as well.

That left only one alternative, she decided as she sat up and started to button her pajama top again. There wasn't any law against sleeping on deck as she'd done before. She could even read by the light on the binnacle until she got in the proper mood.

There was barely a squeak when she opened her cabin door to steal out. It was just as well because a quick glance toward Cole's end of the ship showed that he'd left his own cabin door wide open to catch all the breeze available.

A muffled threshing from there stopped her as she reached the bottom of the stairs and then she relaxed again as she realized that Cole was evidently finding it equally hard to get comfortable on his mattress.

She stole noiselessly up the stairs on bare feet and carefully felt her way to the stern, where she clicked on the tiny binnacle light. With its hood, she didn't have to worry about disturbing Cole in the cabin, and she pulled some of the vinyl cushions into place so that she could achieve a semblance of a bed.

After the first five minutes she could have told the innerspring mattress manufacturers that they didn't have anything to worry about in competition. At least, the temperature was right, and since the moon had emerged from the thready cloud cover for the time being, she was given a clear view of the anchorage.

She let her glance wander around the *Bagatelle*'s neighbors after discovering it was hard to keep her attention on her book when reading in such dim light. By then, all of the cabin illumination was gone from the nearest sloops, showing that the yacht owners had decided on fairly early hours. As she watched, the *Bagatelle* turned in the current. That brought the fifty-one-foot sloop on the starboard side considerably closer than she had remembered before darkness fell.

Could it be that they weren't tied firmly to the buoy, after all? Or perhaps the buoy itself was shifting. Her book thudded onto the deck, completely forgotten in the event of this new happening. And not only new, an inner voice was telling her, downright dangerous. If the *Bagatelle* drifted into the fifty-one footer, God knows what would happen when they collided.

That possibility was so appalling that she didn't hesitate any longer. Jumping to her feet, she pounded down the stairs to the forward cabin.

"Cole, wake up," she said urgently, bending over him where he lay spread-eagled on the mattress, the sheet kicked down by his ankles. "We're drifting—I'm sure of it. Come and see."

He let out a groan, and then, as her words registered, he raised up on the bunk with a muttered curse. "We're what?" he asked, squinting as she switched on his tiny cabin lamp.

"We're drifting."

"We can't be," he countered, and then, focusing on her worried face, he swung his legs onto the floor. "Okay. Simmer down. I'll take a look. Aren't you coming?"

The last came when he looked over his shoulder and discovered she was still in his stateroom.

"I was looking for your robe." She responded before she had a chance to think how it sounded. But the expression that transformed Cole's face showed his reaction immediately.

"My God, it's a good thing you weren't on the *Titanic*. You'd still have been reading the emergency directions on your cabin door when the last lifeboat had shoved off."

"I just thought—" Stephanie had the sense not to say any more since he'd already moved hastily on up the stairs. It wouldn't enhance her reputation to announce that she'd thought he might be cold on deck wearing only pajama bottoms. She shook her head, trying to put her thinking process back into a functioning gear and followed him on deck.

Cole had gone up to the bow when she reached the stern cockpit. She saw that he was holding a flashlight and bending down to check their mooring line. She stayed by the wheel, subsiding on the bench where she'd been trying to sleep earlier.

It wasn't long until Cole was back in the stern replacing the flashlight in a nearby locker with a precise motion that indicated he was having trouble hiding annoyance.

Stephanie waited until he straightened and then asked hesitantly, "Aren't you going to do anything?"

"What did you have in mind?"

"Well, we *are* drifting, aren't we?"

He shook his head. "No, thank God. Everything's just the way it was."

"But it looked as if we were definitely closer to that sloop over there," she countered, and then frowned as she tried to calculate the distance between the two craft. "Well, maybe not now, but earlier I could have sworn . . ." Her voice trailed off under his scrutiny.

"It's deceptive at night. Sometimes the currents make things look different, too. But take my word for it—we're not drifting." He started for the stairs and then paused at the top. "How did it happen that you were up here in the first place?"

"I couldn't sleep down below, so I thought I'd try it on deck."

He retraced his steps then and picked up the book she'd dropped in her haste. "Don't tell me you were trying to read by the binnacle?"

Stephanie didn't care for his barely hidden amusement. "It wasn't too bad," she said stiffly. "I'm sorry I disturbed you."

"So am I." He tried to glance at his watch in the gloom and then shook his head. "I must have been asleep for all of ten minutes." The announcement was punctuated by a mammoth yawn that he made no attempt to hide. "I'll go down and try for ten more if you're happy about the state of the world in general."

"I'm very sorry to have disturbed you." Her tone could have iced fish.

"Oh, hell," he said, wearily rubbbing the back of his neck. "It's been a lousy day. Your head's okay, isn't it?"

Her lips curved reluctantly. "I wasn't seeing things, if that's what you mean."

"Okay. I don't blame you for trying to cool off, but it's getting better all the time down below, so you might feel like moving back to a more comfortable bed later on." A wry expression crossed his face. "At least, it's supposed to be more comfortable. I think the mattress of mine must be almost an inch thick and the vinyl covering ensures that you wake up in a pool of water. It's a good thing these pajamas are drip-dry. See you in the morning."

Chapter 6

Stephanie stared after his disappearing figure and then chuckled slightly as she sat down by the wheel again. Cole hadn't come right out and said that the pajamas were strictly for her benefit, but there wasn't any doubt they were. She sighed and pulled another cushion behind her, trying to stretch out and get comfortable. He was right about finding a better spot to spend the rest of the night, too. Perhaps a little longer up in the breeze and then she'd see if her cabin had cooled off in the interval.

She closed her eyes and made a pronounced effort to relax. Certainly she'd like to forget she'd made a colossal idiot of herself over a false alarm.

Her relaxation technique must have worked because the next time she opened her eyes a considerable time had passed. She knew that from the cooler temperature and her stiff neck, which showed a vinyl deck cushion wasn't an acceptable substitute for feathers or down.

She shivered suddenly, aware that her pajamas weren't keeping her warm at all. In fact, the muggy atmosphere of the cabin suddenly sounded attractive because the zephyrlike breeze that had been so delightful earlier had changed to one with more authority. Stephanie rubbed her arms as she stood up and stretched, trying to ignore her aching neck. The moon was flirting with the cloud cover again, but at that moment it chose to come out of hiding, giving her a clear view of the harbor.

Her gaze went around absently and then she gasped in horror. The big sloop that she'd thought was too close when she called Cole on deck was definitely in danger range now. The *Bagatelle* was easing closer on a collision course with every gust of wind.

Stephanie didn't hesitate. She made a dive for the starter button, hoping prayerfully that the engine would catch on the first try.

For once, things worked in her favor, and the muted roar of the powerful motor was like a symphony to her ears. With one hand on the wheel, she used the other to push the throttle to full power and, a moment later, the *Bagatelle* responded. Even then, she feared she'd left it too late as the stern of the sloop almost brushed the fifty-one-footer riding at anchor. Stephanie thought she saw the twitch of a cabin curtain as she pointed the bow into the wind and steered for a passageway between the anchored yachts.

"What in the devil's going on?" Cole erupted so fast from the companionway that he tripped on the top step and almost measured his length in front of her. His instep must have suffered because he swore again, tightening the belt on his pajama bottoms as he struggled to regain his balance. "Are you out of your mind?" he bit out tersely, seeing her tense figure at the wheel.

"I may be a little flaky, but there's nothing wrong with my eyesight," she snapped back, glad that she had a sounding board for the sheer terror that was just starting to recede. "Even I know that three feet isn't enough clearance between boats, so I thought we'd better get out of there." She jerked her head back in the direction of the big sloop, which was now alight and had two crew members up on deck. "It's a good thing we're too far away to hear what they're saying."

Cole raked a hand through his hair and turned back to her after gazing over the stern. "You mean . . ." He swallowed and started again, his voice deeper than usual. "You mean, we were adrift?"

"We'd have to be, wouldn't we?" she replied, secretly pleased that for once *he* was at a disadvantage. "Otherwise, we wouldn't be going on a joyride around the harbor now. Incidentally, I wish you'd take over and park this thing." Her voice became thready as reaction was setting in with a vengeance.

He gave an extra tug at his pajama belt and said, "You're doing all right. We don't have to worry about the channel in here. Just head for some of that open water ahead while I check our line. I don't see how in the hell that could have worked loose."

He was still talking to himself as he strode quickly up to the bow and got down on his knees, leaning over the side again.

Stephanie glanced upward, giving silent thanks that the moon was clearly visible for a moment as the storm clouds drifted out toward the Atlantic. She throttled down, seeing no need to hurry now that they were safely out of traffic.

Cole was back a few minutes later, saying tersely, "I'll take over," as he edged her away from the wheel.

She watched him spin it and head back toward the main part of the sound. "What are you going to do?" she asked. There was such a grim look on his face that she thought twice about questioning him.

"Find a place where we won't be disturbed, and anchor for the rest of the night."

"You mean we're not going back to The Bitter End moorage?" she queried as she saw him spin the wheel to port rather than toward the lighted resort area.

"That's right." He bit off the words so forcefully she was surprised his jaw didn't crack in the process.

There was a moment of silence and then she decided she was tired of being diplomatic. "Why not?" she asked equally annoyed. "There must be another buoy we could tie up to. They can't all be faulty."

"There wasn't anything wrong with where we were," Cole said, keeping his glance straight ahead. "That mooring line was cut clean through. We were set adrift quite deliberately."

She stared at him, aghast. "You have to be kidding. Who would do a stupid thing like that?"

"Maybe the same person who decided to send you headfirst into a palm tree on Peter Island." He turned his head slightly to give her a narrow-eyed glance. "I'm beginning to believe that old superstition about women on a ship being bad luck."

"That's ridiculous, and you know it," she said. "You can't blame me for some crazy idiot floating around the neighborhood."

" 'Floating' being the operative word in this case. You didn't happen to hear anything before you started this rescue operation, did you?"

There wasn't too much of his expression visible in the dim light of the binnacle, but Stephanie could see enough to realize that he was dead serious in his questioning. She tried to think back. "I'm not sure," she admitted finally. "There probably was some noise, but I can't put a finger on it. At the time, I thought it was possibly because I just got too cold or a crick in my neck." She reached up to rub her nape absently as she spoke. "There could have been the sound of a motor, I suppose."

"Or oars," Cole supplied grimly. "I doubt if our friend would have risked the noise of an outboard, and it was a long swim from shore."

"Whoever it was could have come from one of the yachts nearby."

"It's possible."

The way he said it made Stephanie realize he wouldn't have put his money on it, almost as if he knew that wasn't the way it happened. She shivered suddenly, aware that the breeze was something to be reckoned with as Cole pointed the *Bagatelle*'s bow out into the darkened sound.

He must have been watching her more closely than she'd thought because he said, "You'd better put some clothes on. Or head for the cabin and go to bed. You might as well get some sleep."

She stared at him incredulously. "Are you trying to be funny?"

The quelling glance he shot her way showed that humor was the farthest thing from his mind just then. "What makes you think so?"

She gestured helplessly. "Just that you think I could go calmly down and close my eyes after all that's happened. Besides, I'm not the only person short on clothes. That outfit of yours is a little brief, too."

He looked down, as if just then aware that his

pajama trousers were faithfully outlining his lower half. "I'm sorry if it bothers you," he told her in a tone that showed nothing of the kind. "Right now, I think I'd better stay at the wheel unless you've improved at reading channel markers."

He knew damned well she hadn't, Stephanie thought rebelliously. As a matter of fact, she hadn't even given their route across the lonely water a second thought. "I'll go get you a jacket," she said. "We could probably use some coffee, too."

He uttered a brief snort of laughter. "Women! Talk about ignoring the obvious. I'm surprised you didn't come down and politely ask if you could start the engine when you discovered we were adrift."

"I didn't think of it," she told him with saccharine sweetness that was intended to make his jaw even tighter. "Excuse me, I'll go down now and live up to my reputation."

She could feel his glance on her as she deliberately lingered on the cabin stairs, but once she reached the bottom, she didn't waste any time going to the forward cabin and unhooking a white poplin zipper jacket from the back of the door, taking it back with her. She only went halfway back up the stairs that time, managing to toss it up to him with a careless gesture. She retreated before he could say anything and took refuge in her cabin. Hurriedly unearthing a pair of lightweight jeans, she pulled them on over her pajama pants and topped the combination with a nylon jacket to protect her against the cool wind.

She snatched up a pair of canvas shoes and returned to the galley, putting on the kettle before slipping her bare feet in the shoes and lacing them. While the kettle heated, she took a minute to glance in the mirror and run a comb through her tousled hair. She shrugged at the result before tossing the comb back on the counter. Sailboats brought on a windblown look and there was no use fighting it.

By then, it was time to spoon instant coffee in the mugs and pour in the boiling water. A moment later, she was carrying the steaming cups up the stairs and handing one to Cole.

She noticed as he took it that he'd put on his jacket, so apparently he wasn't going to be too stiff-necked for the rest of the crossing.

In fact, he sounded almost amused as he watched her take a sip of coffee. "I gather that you're determined to stay awake for the rest of the night. You may be sorry in the morning."

She took her time, trying to find a comfortable place on the cushion alongside the wheel. "I'd hate to miss any of the action. Is it a secret where we're going or could I be trusted to know that much?"

He shrugged and then said simply, "I thought we'd tie up at the pier in Leverick Bay until daylight. It's easier than trying to anchor in the dark and far enough away to discourage any more hanky-panky tonight."

Stephanie kept her glance averted, seemingly intent on her steaming coffee. "Have you changed your mind and decided that maybe I'm not the primary target on this cruise?"

His head came up quickly at that. "What are you talking about?"

"Look, I may have my limitations. I know that Dennis Connors won't ever come calling and Julia Child would throw up her hands, but I can figure out a few elementary things. If this is a pleasure cruise, I'm the Queen of Sheba, so why don't you stop hiding behind that stiff male pride of yours and give me some idea of what's going on. After tonight, I think I'm sort of entitled."

He gave her a considering look. "You've got a point. I haven't even thanked you for avoiding that collision and maybe a lot worse back there."

"I don't want any thanks," she said firmly. "But I would like to know the game plan so I can figure out the rules."

"Okay. I'm supposed to be doing surveillance. You were brought along because I thought it would make the *Bagatelle*'s appearance on the scene more plausible. You know, love blooming on the hot tropic nights during a holiday cruise. Apparently the script wasn't convincing enough."

"That isn't surprising," she said, not hiding her disdain. "If you'd told me that I was supposed to be breathing heavily in the close-ups, I might have done better. And aside from that one kiss you gave me at the dock in Road Town, you haven't been steaming up the portholes either. You didn't even . . ." Her voice dropped suddenly. "Wait a minute! Was Nevil the one you were trying to impress?"

"Let's just say that he has an interesting background and being a checkout skipper gives him an excuse for going all over the islands."

"All over the islands doing what?" she asked, taking his mug from him when he drained it.

"We're not exactly sure. All the authorities know is that the Virgin chain has recently become part of the pipeline smuggling contraband from South America. They have reason to believe that the cargo comes in the British Virgins and then is somehow funneled into the American side. Once the stuff reaches St. Thomas, there's no problem getting it to an American mainland port. The risks are taken down here, but it's hard for the customs people to cover all the nooks and crannies among the islands. Especially since this is one of the most popular boating areas in the world. You saw all those sloops lined up at the marina in Road Town, and that doesn't begin to cover the power cruisers or the rest of the islands."

"But where do you come into this? And me, for heaven's sake?"

"I overheard a strange conversation when I was down in this part of Gorda Sound earlier this year. Since my company does business in St. Thomas, I thought I'd better alert the authorities there. They passed me on to the British officials on Tortola, who hoped a return cruise might pay off. Everybody seemed to think that one more American tourist wouldn't arouse any suspicion—especially on a sailing holiday. Unfortunately my crew choice had to cancel at the last minute, but then you appeared on the scene. That was a plus."

Stephanie ignored the last part of his sentence. "What happened to her?"

"Who?"

"The woman who was your first choice."

"It was supposed to be a policewoman, but they couldn't find the right candidate." He rubbed the side of his nose reflectively. "There was some mix-up in the scheduling."

Which didn't really explain anything, Stephanie thought, giving him an annoyed look. She knew all along that she'd been a last-minute selection; it hadn't occurred to her that she was a substitute for another woman.

"I must have slipped up somewhere along the line," Cole admitted. "There was a possibility that first attack on Peter Island could have been an accident. You know, where the innocent victim just happens to walk by at the wrong time." He paused to check his bearings in the channel and then went on, almost as if thinking aloud. "But setting us adrift tonight puts paid to that theory. I'll report in tomorrow and see what my next move is supposed to be. It's possible they've changed the timetable as well."

Stephanie didn't like the way he was saying

"I" instead of "we," but she decided it wasn't the right time to mention it. Instead, she tried a different tack. "You mentioned that your company does business in St. Thomas. Does that mean you're connected with the authorities in some way?"

"Lord, no. You see before you a struggling American businessman who's just trying to stay ahead of the competition."

He would make a very good lawman, Stephanie decided, since extracting information from him was like digging for gold in the Yukon; there was a lot of extraneous material to be sifted through before reaching paydirt.

"At least it isn't interfering with your social life," she said, trying to sound as if she really didn't care. "How were the goings-on at The Bitter End tonight?"

There was that pause again, as if he were deciding just how much to say. "The bar was crowded, but then it usually is. I hope to hell that there's space to tie up at Leverick."

"Couldn't you check by radio?"

"I could. I could also send up flares to let everybody around know we're coming, but I'd rather not. We'll find out sooner or later."

Stephanie ignored his sarcasm, belatedly aware that he'd changed the subject again hoping that she'd follow the red herring. Instead, she went back to her questioning. "You didn't mention how you happened to be on such close terms with the authorities down here. Weren't they pretty skeptical when you reported your suspicions?"

Even in the dim light, she could see the wry expression that crossed his features. "I didn't say they welcomed me with open arms. On the other hand, they didn't want to overlook any possibility. And adding one operative in the area was hardly a project for the joint chiefs of staff. As I already knew Ian, he provided the official clout."

"Ian. You mean the man you were talking with at The Bitter End earlier?"

"That's right." Cole took one hand off the wheel to knead the top of his shoulder, as if a muscle pained him.

Stephanie was still trying to put the man she'd met earlier in uniform and found it hard going. "He didn't look like a policeman," she said finally.

"He isn't required to wear a badge on a sport shirt."

Stephanie shot him a quelling look. "That isn't what I meant. As a matter of fact, you don't fit into the category of a struggling businessman either."

"Look, what *is* this?" Cole's voice had lost any vestige of humor. "Are you doing a survey for the IRS or what?"

"After tonight, you can't blame me for wanting to ask a few questions," she countered.

"I thought I'd answered more than a few. If you want to check my passport, it's down in my locker. There's a business card in the case, too. I

represent a company that handles security in-
stallations for industrial concerns. It's a family
firm, but don't get the idea that I didn't have to
work at it. My grandfather believed in everybody starting at the bottom. Anyhow, that's the
reason I know more than my share of law-
enforcement people. When we take on a job
anywhere in the world, the authorities expect to
be alerted on all the new security wrinkles we're
installing. And now that you've been clued in
on everything, I suggest that you go below and
try to get some sleep for the rest of the night."

"I promise I will as soon as we tie up. I'm still
a little jittery." Her voice wavered and then she
gathered her courage. "I'm sorry if you thought
I was nosy."

"Forget it." He rubbed his shoulder again.
"This whole damned idea has backfired. I was a
fool to get you involved in the first place."

"You didn't have much of a choice once I
came aboard."

"That's true." A ghost of a smile flickered
over his tired face. "You do bear a certain re-
semblance to a barnacle."

"I've never been called that before. Would
you like me to get you some more coffee?" she
asked, hoping to make amends.

"No, thanks. You can keep me awake for the
rest of the crossing with *your* life story, since
this seems to be confession time. I must say I
was a little surprised to find somebody like you
floating around the marina back on Tortola."

"You make me sound like a camp follower," she said, her voice rising angrily.

"Hardly. After the first two minutes you cleared the slate of that idea. I was still surprised that you came along."

"Well, after the first two minutes, you came through my test with flying colors," she mimicked, relaxing again. "I'm not sure why. Probably it was because you were so careful to explain that there was absolutely nothing personal in the invitation and for me not to get the wrong idea."

"Which shows that the best of intentions can go awry. How was I to know that you'd be running into a palm tree within four or five hours?"

Stephanie's pulse rate accelerated at his first comment but it calmed down again at his last one. What he meant was that he'd been pressed into service as a nursemaid ever since, and from his tone, it wasn't the role he would have chosen.

"What's on the agenda for tomorrow?" she asked after the pause between them had lengthened.

"I'll use the phone ashore and see what the newest orders are. At least you won't have to worry on this side of Gorda Sound. I'm sure that if our chum Nevil is still around, he has more important things on his mind."

Stephanie knew that his comment was meant to be reassuring, but it didn't do much for her ego. Even Nevil, it seemed, wouldn't be interested in the first mate of the *Bagatelle* if she didn't intrude on his stamping ground. "Damn," she muttered.

"What's that?"

"Nothing. I broke a nail," she said, improvising hastily. She glanced ahead of them to where the lights of a small marina could be seen against a dark hillside. "Is that Leverick Bay?"

"That's right. Drake's Anchorage is off to port. There's a pretty strong current running there, so we'll do it the simple way and tie up to a pier tonight if there's space available. There should be some deckhand around to handle the lines. I don't think I'd better trust you with the wheel under these conditions."

"It wouldn't be a good idea. The way things have been going, I'd probably take out half the pier on my first approach." She got to her feet a few minutes later saying, "I'll handle the bow line if there isn't any hired help around."

"Okay, but be careful. Make sure you don't jump down to the pier until we're almost dead in the water alongside. Have you got that?"

"I understand," she called back over her shoulder as she carefully made her way along the narrow deck past the cabin area. If only he had a little more confidence in her ability, she thought wistfully. It was surprising that he hadn't pinned a note on her shirt when she went ashore so that she'd be able to find her way back to the boat.

"Ready with your bow?"

His sharp call brought her back to the present, and she hurried to pick up the neatly coiled nylon line. "I have it," she told him.

"Okay. It looks clear on the outer pier. I'll come about and cut my speed. Wait until I signal before you go ashore."

Fortunately there was some illumination so that the outlines of the dock were visible. Cole swung the *Bagatelle* wide and then throttled down.

He'd done it too soon, Stephanie thought, peering anxiously over the bow as they approached. Then, surprisingly they were alongside and she looked back to the stern for instructions.

Cole was at the rail making sure of their position as he started to put over the rubber fenders. "Okay," he called to her. "Get your line on that buoy by the storage locker. Now," he added in a tone that had her over the side of the *Bagatelle* in a instant.

Fortunately it wasn't much of a drop down to the dock, and after a slight stagger to reclaim her balance, she was tying up as he'd instructed. She looked back then, aware for the first time that Cole had jumped onto the dock himself to fasten the stern line. That accomplished, he came up to check on her and gave a satisfied nod.

He glanced around the deserted dock afterward, saying in some surprise, "I thought they'd have a guard out to make sure somebody doesn't run off with the place."

Stephanie tried to see the dial of her watch. "At three A.M., he could be taking a break. Besides, there's not much around here to steal," she said, gesturing at the wooden pier. "Most of the stuff over there at the marina seems to be under lock and key." She peered up toward the hillside attempting to identify a small cluster of buildings. "Is that a hotel?"

"I think so." He tried to hide a yawn. "Unless things have changed in the last month or so. It's a little late to find out if there's any room in the inn. We'd better spend what's left of the night on board. At least, you won't have to worry about drifting this time."

She nodded solemnly and accepted his boost back up to the *Bagatelle*'s deck. " 'S funny," she said as they made their way to the cabin stairs, "the wind seems to have dropped again."

"Because we're in a protected harbor."

"Of course. That makes sense." She moved wearily down the steps, feeling for the first time as if it were the middle of the night. Unfortunately the air in the cabin hadn't cooled perceptibly and she could have groaned as she stepped into her stuffy stateroom. She wondered for an instant if sleeping on deck would be acceptable, and then decided against it. If a security guard came down to check on them, she didn't want to be the one receiving in a pair of pajamas.

"Something wrong?" Cole asked from the middle of the cabin.

"No. No, of course not." She managed a smile and started to close her stateroom door.

"You'll regret that." Cole's laconic comment stopped her halfway. "There won't be any air for you if you close the door. That's why I'm going to doss down out here." He was moving some of their supplies from the side bench of the dining area as he spoke, and then reached up to open the ceiling hatch. "This should get all the breeze that's going. Incidentally, these cushions make into a pretty good-size bunk, so you're welcome to share. Just bring a pillow. You sure as hell won't need a blanket."

"Oh, no." Stephanie's refusal was automatic as she watched him tug the last long bench cushion into place. "I'll be fine in my cabin, thanks. Maybe I will leave the door open, though."

"Whatever you want," he replied off-handedly. "G'night."

Stephanie closed her cabin door long enough to shed her jeans and jacket, which suddenly felt like a suit of armor. "Damn," she muttered, and debated for a good fifteen seconds whether to root around in her things and find a robe. When she felt perspiration starting to run between her breasts, she abandoned the idea of any more clothes. Cole certainly was no stranger to the scantily clad female form. She hadn't dwelled on how she'd been arrayed in the sleep shirt at Peter Island because it was easier to ignore the whole thing. Like the Victorian brides who, when confronted with their conjugal duties, were instructed to close their eyes and think of England. Stephanie felt a rivulet of perspiration start to trickle down her back and made up her mind. If she stayed in her stateroom much longer, she'd go topless, so now was the time to get some air. She switched on the fan, wincing at its noisy whine before going back into the main cabin.

There was the sound of movement behind the doors in the bow, which showed that Cole was following roughly the same schedule. She darted into the tiny stern head and firmly closed the door behind her. It wasn't quite as hot as her stateroom, she decided as she punched open the tiny hatch, but it wasn't great. After this, she must remember not to recommend a bare-boat cruise anywhere for a honeymoon couple. Between the stifling cabin, the pitfalls of the galley, and the perils of navigation, most couples would be lucky to make it to the first port before debarking to find a good lawyer.

At least there wouldn't be any need for that with Cole, she decided. They'd part after exchanging telephone numbers and a polite handshake. And if she'd stayed there much longer thinking such cheerful thoughts, she'd have to put her head under the faucet and turn on what was supposed to be the cold water.

She flipped off the light and opened the door to step boldly out into what was now a dark cabin. Before she got her bearings, she knocked something heavy from the nearby locker and heard it hit the floor. An instant later, a side light was switched on by Cole, who'd raised up from his bed in the middle of the room like a weary phoenix emerging from the ashes.

"It's okay. I can find my way," Stephanie heard herself babbling as she hastened toward her room. "I'm sorry to wake you up."

"Since I'd only turned out the light thirty seconds ago, it's no big deal. I'll leave it on until you're safely settled." He watched her go in her stateroom and hurriedly switch off the tiny fan, which, by then, sounded like a giant mosquito.

"You'll need that for ventilation," he said reluctantly.

"I doubt if even a Buddhist monk could tune out that noise," she told him. "If I leave the door open, I'll be all right. G'night."

He reached up and turned off the light, not bothering with any more amenities.

Stephanie heard the creak of vinyl as he stretched out again, and she tried to do the same thing on her thin mattress. From then on, things went steadily downhill. The upper sheet lasted for a bare five minutes before she kicked it off. Two minutes later, she rose on an elbow to try to punch a hole in a pillow made of leftover anchor parts. Hot anchor parts, she decided after putting her nose down on it again. Perhaps it would be better if she tried lying on her back and let the back of her head get hot. She flopped over again, and that time only succeeded in getting the discarded upper sheet wound around her feet. "Damn and blast," she muttered. She tried kicking with one foot to dislodge it and then both feet, unaware that her activity came complete with sound effects. That became evident an instant later when the cabin lamp clicked on and Cole's feet hit the floor.

"I don't know what you're doing in here, but it sounds like an elephant stampede," he snapped as he came to loom over her cabin threshold. "Apparently there's only one way that either of us is going to get any sleep for the rest of the night." He bent over to lift her bodily and marched back to the main cabin, where he dropped her on the edge of his bed. "I don't care which side you choose," he announced then, "providing you keep quiet and hold still. Understand?"

Stephanie, who was poised to stomp off, took another look at his face and decided against it. "Okay," she muttered, "but you didn't have to be such a bast—" She swallowed and changed her noun, "Such a pill about it." By then she'd scuttled to the far side of the mattress, appropriating one of his pillows on the way.

Cole's angry glance held her defiant one for a moment longer. Then he reached over to switch off the lamp and lowered himself onto the other side of the mattress.

The silence that followed was almost eerie. Stephanie knew that she was holding herself so rigidly that she could have passed for a case of rigor mortis. Finally Cole let out an exasperated sigh as he turned toward her.

"I didn't mean that you aren't allowed to breath every five minutes or so," he commented dryly.

She rolled back to face him, although staying carefully on her side of the mattress. "I can't seem to please you with anything I do."

"Don't be a fool. We might be sharing a bed, but that doesn't mean you have to worry about my pouncing on you as soon as you close your eyes. You can put your pillow down the middle if it bothers you."

"You're the one who's complaining," she told him indignantly. "Go ahead and use your own pillow."

"The hell with that."

"There's no need to be unpleasant." She took a delight in pursuing the subject, since it seemed to irritate him so much. "Maybe you could find a substitute."

"The only thing within reach is a loaf of bread," he said, evidently looking around. "Would that make you feel better?"

"I feel fine," she snapped. "And I'm certainly not going to sleep with a loaf of bread."

"My feelings exactly, but that's my best and only offer."

She watched his shadowy outline turn over again, aware for the first time that he hadn't bothered about an upper sheet when he'd made the bed. Presumably he thought that a pair of pajama bottoms was all that was necessary for gracious living. Certainly for shared living. It would serve him right if she'd insisted on a loaf of bread, she thought, and had trouble smothering a giggle at the prospect. Then she realized that she'd been so busy getting annoyed that she'd forgotten to be nervous.

It was silly to give their shared accommodations another thought. All she had to do was stay on her side of the bed and everything would be fine. Cole's deep, relaxed breathing showed that he wasn't lying awake thinking about the propriety of the situation. She yawned and then buried her face deeper in the pillow, letting her eyelids flicker once and then go down to stay.

Chapter 7

There was a wonderful smell. Stephanie settled even deeper into her pillow, sleepily aware that it must be a splendid dream to come equipped with such extras.

She thought about opening her eyes to check on the time and then decided against it. After all, it had been very late, or early, before she'd gotten to sleep. She stretched luxuriously on the mattress, wondering how she could ever have thought the cabin of the *Bagatelle* wouldn't be comfortable.

It took a few seconds for that thought to penetrate and then her eyes opened wide as the memories came flooding back.

There was just dim light in the cabin but her startled glance took in the bright sunlight edging the curtains drawn over the portholes. She pushed up on an elbow then and saw to her horror that she was on Cole's side of the mattress. She flopped over quickly, only to discover that Cole hadn't been forced to play musical beds in the middle of the night; she was the sole occupant.

An ominous crackling by her hip brought her upright and she let out a startled shriek at the strange shape cuddled next to her.

She was out on the floor before she looked back to see if it had followed her. Then there was a burst of laughter nearby as she identified her bedside companion.

"Bread," she said with loathing, and picked it up to throw at Cole, who was convulsed with amusement at the bottom of the stairs.

"Hold it," he ordered, putting up an authoritative hand to stop her in her tracks. "That's breakfast. Along with coffee. Unless you want to wait until the dining room opens in the hotel."

Stephanie lowered the loaf reluctantly. "Okay, you win. But it was a dirty trick. I thought it was a rat, at first. Oh, I know it isn't the right size," she added when his eyebrows climbed, "but I barely had my eyes open."

"If you'd waited a little longer, I was going to serve you coffee in bed," Cole announced, pushing back the curtains and then unwrapping the bread to take out two slices. "This is the time to brush your teeth and all the amenities. Breakfast will be served on deck in about five minutes."

"But you're dressed and everything," Stephanie said, stopping on her way toward the stern to fix him with an accusing eye. He had changed into clean jeans and a white T-shirt that showed the wiry fitness of his tall frame and enhanced his tanned skin. His hair was still damp but neatly combed, and only the lines around his eyes showed that he could have used some more sleep.

"Put on a robe if you want, but you don't have to worry—those pajamas of yours would make about twenty-five bikinis," he observed, yawning, and then turned to the stove to pour a cup of coffee.

Apparently the discussion was finished, Stephanie decided irritably, but found herself snatching up a thigh-length robe in her stateroom before going to the head.

She just managed to wash her face, brush her teeth, and do a "lick and a promise" with a comb to get on deck within the five-minute interval.

Cole nodded approvingly and said, "Sit down and I'll bring your food up. Want jam on your toast?"

"Yes, please." She thought about offering to help and then decided against it. After all, she might as well enjoy things while she could.

It was going to be a pretty day, she decided, taking a quick look around the moorage before settling on a cushion near the wheel. There weren't many people stirring in the marina yet, but she could see a delivery truck pull up to the small hotel on the hillside and a gardener was attacking weeds at the side of a road that curved between vacation homes. It would be a nice place to spend a holiday, Stephanie thought. There was a splendid view over the blue waters of Gorda Sound, and far out to sea there was the gentle outline of Necker Island. She stood up to peer over the bow of the *Bagatelle* to check the distance they'd covered after leaving The Bitter End, and sat down again, trying not to remember the danger that had preceded it. It was better to enjoy the morning sunlight and the gentle breeze, which just barely made waves lap against the schooner's hull.

She saw Cole at the bottom of the stairs and went over to take her coffee mug from him and a paper plate of buttered toast.

"I'll bring the jam," he said. "Just go and sit down. If you want any juice, sing out now."

"Forget it. I'll have it for dessert," she told him as she carried her breakfast back to the stern. "I must say, this loaf of bread has certainly served a multitude of roles," she told him solemnly when he sat down, depositing the jam jar and spoon between them.

"Hasn't it?" He was having trouble keeping a sober expression. "The look on your face when you found it in bed will be hard to top."

"There must be a special place in hell for people who pull practical jokes at the crack of dawn," she said austerely.

He kept his glance on the jam jar as he spread a piece of toast generously and then passed it to her. "I just thought there should be some compensation for the rest of the night."

His comment seemed to hang in the air while Stephanie suddenly remembered that she'd been on his side of the mattress when she awoke. That could mean that he'd had to get up with the birds as a matter of self-preservation. It would have been better if he'd simply given her a polite shove, rather than making a snide remark.

She took another bite of toast, thinking suddenly that it tasted like flavored cardboard and was just as difficult to swallow. After one or two attempts, she tossed it overboard, saying, "I never eat much breakfast. The coffee tastes good, though. What's our schedule for today?"

Cole was methodically working through his pile of toast. Insomnia hadn't affected his appetite, Stephanie thought despondently. "I'd like to get out of here pretty soon," he was saying between bites. "It isn't far to Drake's Anchorage and I've arranged to rent a cottage there. You'll like it—there's a nice beach with a decent runoff and some good walking trails on the hill behind the resort."

"You're beginning to sound like a travel folder," Stephanie said, her eyes hooded against the sun as she surveyed him. "What is it that makes me suspicious? I thought we were taking a cruise."

"I told you there might be a change of plans."

He was concentrating on the piece of toast in his hand. "Unfortunately, this latest decision doesn't include you. I'll give things a day or two, and then, if it looks as if the plan is dragging on too long, I'll send you back to Road Town. Or, if you'd rather, I could arrange passage for you today."

His tone was so flat and decisive that Stephanie knew it wouldn't do any good to argue. She swallowed hard, fighting the tears that threatened to overflow, and stared fixedly at the mug in her hand. "I think I'll get a little more coffee," she said, keeping her head averted as she started toward the stairs.

"Wait a minute." His command halted her halfway down, but she kept her back to him so that he wouldn't see the tears coursing her cheeks. "Are you willing to be parked at Drake's for the moment?" he asked, his voice still hard and unyielding.

"If that's what you want," she said, proud of her level response.

"Okay. Then you'd better pack your things while you're below. I'll go ahead and cast off. There isn't any time to lose."

When Stephanie came on deck later, she'd changed into a pair of emerald-green shorts and a matching sport shirt with a white collar and cuffs. She'd pulled her hair back from her face with a chiffon scarf and donned a pair of sunglasses to hide any evidence of her earlier tears.

She was surprised to see how far they'd traveled, and then noticed that Cole hadn't bothered with the sails but was content to use the motor on this leg across the sound.

"All packed?" he asked, showing he hadn't relented while she'd been below.

"All packed." She kept her gaze fixed on the small island they were approaching. "This is certainly the quiet end of the sound. Other than those few buildings along the shore, it doesn't look as if there's any other habitation."

"Maybe Mosquito Island doesn't have the general appeal of some other places, but it should be secure for you. Besides, a little rest and quiet will be appropriate after all that's happened. There's a good restaurant at the Landing, too, so food won't be a problem."

Stephanie could have told him it wasn't a lack of food that was bothering her. The knowledge that he wasn't going to be around was the only drawback in her thoughts just then, but she had no intention of admitting it. She kept her attention fixedly on one long wharf and the small harbor where five or six schooners still rode at anchor.

Cole was going on, "I've arranged to take care of all your expenses here, so you won't have to worry about your budget."

"That wasn't necessary," she said, giving him a fleeting glance over her shoulder. "I'm perfectly able to pay my own way."

She heard him mutter something unprintable before he said, "Forget it. You've come out on the short end of this trip all the way along. The least I can do is provide a little rest and relaxation."

A frown creased her forehead as she turned to ask, "When did you make all these arrangements?"

"This morning. There was a phone on the wharf at Leverick Bay. You were still asleep." The last was added almost reluctantly.

While he was busy making plans to get rid of her, Stephanie thought as Cole throttled down to come alongside the wooden pier of the resort. There was no sign of life from the cluster of buildings near the dock, but she could see a winding path and a glass-fronted hut that evidently was the restaurant he had mentioned.

"Get the bow line, will you?"

Cole's terse request sent her forward to pick up the coiled rope. By that time, Cole had the *Bagatelle* nearly dead in the water and it was an easy task to step ashore and drop the nylon line over the cleat on the wooden pier.

At the same time, Cole cut the engine and, an instant later, had fastened the stern line. Without saying anything, he disappeared down the cabin steps and reappeared shortly with her luggage. He deposited it on the pier and turned to say, "I'm sorry I don't have time to make sure you're settled in. Just go on down to the office and tell them who you are. They'll send someone to handle your bags and take you to your cottage. I'll be in touch as soon as I can. Wait here until you hear from me. Okay?"

It wasn't the time to argue. Stephanie faced him with dignity and said, "There's no need to worry about me. I'll be fine."

His expression hardened. "That's not the right answer. I want you here, so don't get any bright ideas about going off on your own. Do you understand?"

"You don't have to treat me like a six-year-old—"

He caught her elbow, cutting her off in midsentence. "If you don't promise, you'll be sorry when I do catch up. Now, behave yourself and go have a decent breakfast."

He bent his head to give her a rough but thorough kiss before stepping back aboard the schooner. "Get the bow line, will you?" he commanded, reaching over to thumb the button for the engine.

Stephanie was still dazed and breathing hard, but she managed to toss the line on deck while Cole was taking care of the stern. Her gaze held his for a long moment as he throttled back and pointed the *Bagatelle* toward the middle of Gorda Sound.

After that, she turned to walk slowly along the pier. There was no use waiting and hoping he'd give her a final wave. Cole Warner wasn't the kind of man to look back for any reason. Even his last command that she stick around until he could figure out a polite way to dismiss her from the scene didn't raise her hopes. As for his kiss, it was merely quid pro quo, as her Latin teacher used to say. A compensation in kind because she was too old to be patted on the head.

Her steps slowed because she wanted to make sure that all evidence of the tears streaming down her cheeks was gone by the time she reached the resort office.

Chapter 8

If she had to be put ashore on an island, Stephanie admitted later in the day, Cole had picked a very acceptable one. The cottage she'd been assigned faced the white sandy beach and the blue expanse of Gorda Sound. There was a screened porch if she wanted fresh air, and comfortable chaise longues located down on the sand. The interior of the cottage was pleasant, rattan and green chinz presenting a cool atmosphere with the white walls and ceiling. Television was nonexistent, but there was a bedside radio, and an overhead fan substituted for air-conditioning. On the other hand, lunch consisted of three elaborate courses, and Stephanie had the feeling that she'd gain five pounds within a week if she stayed around. To avoid such a happening, she decided a walk was definitely on the agenda before her late dinner reservation.

She had just reached her screened cottage porch when her attention was caught by a power cruiser anchoring in the protected area north of the wharf. Whoever it was had picked a spot at a considerable distance from the sailboats already anchored for the night. She wondered why, and her curiosity made her linger on the porch as the man on deck jumped into his dinghy and started the motor. There was something familiar about his movements and Stephanie squinted against the glare of the late-afternoon sun on the water trying to decide why. Apparently he wasn't going to oblige her by coming close to the cottage or the resort's main buildings so that she could get a good look.

All she could determine was that he was dark-haired and slim—plus no slouch at handling boats. He'd managed the anchoring with the thoroughness of an old hand as well as maneuvering the dinghy across the cove's strong currents. Even as she watched, he ran the dinghy's bow into the sand on the isolated part of the beach.

Stephanie moved out on her cottage steps, watching him jump onto the sand and quickly pull the small craft farther out of the water. He looked over his shoulder then and instinctively Stephanie drifted on down the steps and turned away from him on a path toward the resort's main buildings. She didn't look back until a clump of shrubbery provided a shield. Then she peered through the leaves of the undergrowth to see him disappearing on the gravel path leading toward the north end of Mosquito Island.

She closed her eyes for an instant, trying to remember the big overall map of the place she'd seen by the registration desk earlier. It had shown all the favorite walking tours for guests, and if she remembered correctly, the path he'd taken was one of the main ones. She frowned thoughtfully and decided it was worth checking out.

A sleepy bellman, lounging by the reservation desk, confirmed it a few minutes later.

"Yes, miss." He nodded as he watched her trace the route on the map. "That does go to Honeymoon Cove on the other side of the island. It's a good walk—a little steep, but you shouldn't have any trouble. There's lots of prickly stuff if you go off the path and a whole hillside full of crabs, but they won't bother you. They're too busy getting out of the way," he finished with a wide grin.

A slight frown went over her face. "Big crabs or little ones?"

He gestured, measuring off two or three inches with his fingers. "About this size."

She smiled back at him. "That I can handle."

He nodded. "It's more important that you don't go too far and miss your dinner reservation. We've a full house tonight and you wouldn't want to go to bed hungry."

"After lunch, that shouldn't happen for a day or so," she advised him.

"Well, if you leave now and just go to the top of the path, you'll be back in time. Besides, if you started down to Honeymoon Cove on the other side, you'd have an awful steep climb back and it's pretty hot for that." His approving glance went over the sunglasses she'd pushed up on her forehead and the brimmed cotton hat she was carrying. "It don't pay to get too much sun in these parts."

"I'll be careful. And I'll be sure to be back for dinner," she told him with a smile.

As she set out on the path that passed her cottage and then intersected the main one for Honeymoon Cove, she was glad she'd told someone where she was going. Not that there was any reason to be nervous, she decided, and she certainly wouldn't hear from Cole. Hoping for that was a mental aberration that couldn't be blamed on too much sun.

She started to grin as she thought of the crab population. Two-inch crabs didn't pose as much of a threat as the mosquitoes she'd heard in her cottage earlier. She hadn't been surprised. There had to be a reason for the Mosquito Island name.

When she came abreast of her cottage, she detoured in to apply some insect repellent. She was going out the door again when she stopped and scrawled a hasty note on the pad atop her bedside table saying that she'd be back soon. Just on the off chance that Cole returned early, it wouldn't hurt to leave a message for him.

"You're an idiot," she told herself firmly as she let herself out the front door. On the other hand, nothing ventured, nothing gained. She left the premises unlocked, too—making sure that there were no barriers in his way.

The sun was low but still hot enough to bring a sheen to her forehead as she started on the main trail. She moved along at a leisurely rate, happy that there wasn't any time limit involved. A glance at the water to her right showed the usual amount of sailboats in the channel farther out, most of them headed for an anchorage at The Bitter End or possibly a pleasant sail even farther up to Biras Creek.

There wouldn't be a lack of people around there, she thought, and frowned slightly as she considered her deserted surroundings. Apparently the guests on Mosquito Island preferred to stay in their cottages until time to gather for food in the main resort building. Aside from two children happily wading in the shallows behind her, there wasn't a vacationer in sight.

The sparse vegetation had been another surprise. From the water, the island seemed to be a velvety green, but once ashore, it proved to be rocky and rugged. The thick undergrowth looked heavier on the hillside ahead of her with an unusual amount of succulents scattered alongside the trail. Nothing like the palm-lined scenery earlier at Peter Island, she thought idly, and rubbed her bruised forehead. Probably that was just as well. A collision with one of the Mosquito Island's cacti would be considerately more painful at the outset.

As she skirted a tidal pool, she noticed that she was almost abreast of the dinghy whose occupant had piqued her curiosity in the first place. She took a few steps toward it, trying to avoid the wet, sloppy sand in that area, and then stopped to look around. If the man came back and found her investigating his property, she'd have a hard time thinking up an excuse. Besides, the dinghy looked remarkably uninteresting. The interior was completely bare except for a paddle clamped to the inside of the craft; an ordinary-looking outboard was pulled up on the stern. Apparently there had once been a number on the bow, but paint had covered everything but the barest outline of that.

So much for detective work, Stephanie decided wryly, and turned back to the path. All she'd gotten out of it was muddy shoes.

It took five minutes of scuffing her soles and trying to scrape the mud off with a handy frond before she could resume her climb. She moved up on the path, which narrowed after leaving the beach until it was finally single-file status. It was at the trail's first switchback that she glimpsed the crabs the bellman had mentioned earlier.

As she moved around a big stone at the side of the path, there was suddenly a whole colony of the small crustaceans on view. Most of them scurried to find cover under the bracken, but a few scuttled bravely up the hillside for other terrain.

Stephanie stood with a bemused smile on her face, observing the comic exodus. As she watched a straggler head for a rock that was just past the toe of her shoe, she was glad that the largest of the crabs seemed to be only three or four inches across.

She lingered for a moment longer, waiting to see if the crabs would reappear, but when the place remained empty, she turned back on the path and continued her upward climb.

The heat increased as she neared the top of the ridge, and her stops became more frequent. She rationalized that she was stopping only to admire the view of Gorda Sound spread out behind her. In reality, she was woefully out of condition, which meant she'd better enroll in a decent exercise program once she got home again.

The crab population appeared on both sides of the path as she went along, and she became accustomed to hearing their scuttling, interspersed with the sound of her footsteps on the loose gravel.

It was as she was finally nearing the top of the ridge that she became careless. Her attention was caught by a crab moving almost alongside, and when it suddenly decided to cross in front of her, she pulled up abruptly. She stepped back to avoid crushing the small creature and inadvertently came down off the edge of the gravel surface onto dirt a few inches below, turning her ankle in the process. She winced with pain as she regained her balance and put her weight on it.

She stood immobile for a moment, trying to decide what to do. The sensible thing was to hop to a nearby rock almost shrouded in undergrowth. She managed to reach it in awkward fashion a second or so later and thankfully collapsed onto it. An overhanging branch made her crouch uncomfortably and there was a bump atop it that felt like a broken bedspring. Even so, it gave her a chance to sit down and enjoy the partial shade while she contemplated her ankle.

A few minutes' rest should help, she concluded after waggling her foot gingerly. Then she'd start back down the path again. It was frustrating to miss the summit of the trail after coming so close, but if the pain in her ankle worsened, she could be in for an overnight stay on the hillside if there weren't any other hikers about.

She decided not to worry about that alarming possibility, choosing instead to try to relax in her stooped position.

It was perhaps five minutes later when she'd just about made up her mind to start out again that the sound of masculine voices above her brought her head up in surprise.

She had opened her mouth to call for assistance when she heard a familiar accent that made her subside rapidly. It seemed impossible that Nevil had changed locales from The Bitter End to the top of a ridge on Mosquito Island, but there was no mistaking his nasal Aussie tones. His presence prompted her to remain under cover, for she had no desire to let him know she was on the island. If only Cole were around, she thought despairingly, aware that something must have gone radically wrong with the surveillance plan. Obviously he and his friend Ian must have thought that Nevil would be at the far end of Gorda Sound and he'd slipped through their net.

It was hard to understand what the two at the top of the path were saying, but their discussion was heated. By craning her head, she could see Nevil gesturing, and the phrase "bloody damned fools" came floating through the early evening.

His companion seemed to be trying to placate him and must have succeeded to a certain extent because Nevil finally said, "Better not try it again if they want to stay in the game."

His companion muttered something she couldn't hear.

Nevil gestured again. "The hell with that," he said. "We'll pick you up tomorrow as arranged."

There was another murmur of protest but Nevil cut off the words abruptly. "I don't care what you do," he said in emphatic tones that penetrated the quiet air. "Count crabs, or birds, or twiddle your thumbs. Just have a good story if somebody comes along, but keep watch in the channel until we weigh anchor. That's why I'm leaving the walkie-talkie with you."

It was obvious that Nevil was about to depart, and Stephanie's pulse bounded. There was no way she could pull back into the shrubbery far enough that he would miss her. She could only hope that she'd be able to think of an acceptable story before he came down the trail.

Her whirling thoughts subsided when she realized there were no approaching footsteps. Nevil had evidently gone down the other side of the path from the ridge, headed toward Honeymoon Cove.

If that was the case, he must have a schooner anchored in the cove to explain his presence on the island. But it didn't sound as if he was going to calmly sail off into the sunset—not if he was leaving his partner on the ridge summit to keep watch. But watch for what?

Stephanie rubbed her damp forehead and tried to ignore the trickle of perspiration that reached her waistband just then. By craning her head, she could see a partial profile of the man Nevil had left on guard. There wasn't enough light to make out any distinguishing features at that distance, and she certainly didn't want to stay in her shrubbery until the darkness fell completely.

Probably the best thing was to beat a careful

retreat and hope to go unnoticed. If caught, she couldn't pretend to be a bird-watcher, since Caribbean pelicans were the only shore birds she could safely identify. Far better to just play the innocuous tourist role since she fit it perfectly. Once she got back to the resort office, she'd try to contact Cole or his friend Ian and spread the word.

The whole scheme sounded about as plausible as hoping to pay her rent with a winning lottery ticket, but there didn't seem to be any viable alternative. One thing sure, she'd better get going before darkness covered the hillside.

Her plan would have worked fine except that she'd forgotten an important factor: after waiting for the man at the summit to turn toward the cove, she stepped hastily onto the path and her strained ankle gave way under her. She slithered in the loose gravel to regain her balance, probably looking like a shore bird herself as she tried to favor her swollen foot.

She heard swift movement on the path above and could have groaned aloud as she saw the man she'd been trying to elude hurrying toward her.

The surprise on his face must have mirrored hers.

"You," he exclaimed. "What are you doing here?"

She tried to think just what she could safely say with one part of her mind while the other half was trying to understand why the manager of the resort where she'd stayed on Tortola should be standing at the summit ridge of Mosquito Island. He even looked incongrous, attired in grubby slacks and sport shirt instead of the natty business suit and crisp white shirt he'd worn at the hotel. "Admiring the scenery, probably the same thing you are," she got out finally. "It's Mr. Stacy, isn't it?"

He stared at her. A deep frown showing that he wasn't pleasantly surprised by her presence brought his eyebrows together. "That's right. I thought you were with Warner."

"Well, I was. For a while." Stephanie's mind was racing as she tried to decide which tack to take so that she could get back down the trail as quickly as possible. "He—he had other plans for the day."

"You mean you've been on this island all day?"

"Actually I slept most of it. You know how it is aboard a sailboat—the accommodations aren't exactly five-star, so I had to make up for lost time." Stephanie was aware that she was chattering, but a giddy female might be the most convincing role. Not that she was having any trouble fitting the part, she thought wryly. She shifted her weight and winced when her swollen ankle gave another twinge.

Stacy was quick to note it. "What's the matter?"

"Nothing much." She gestured airily. "I just twisted my ankle on this loose gravel a little while ago. That's why I was resting—to see if it would get better."

The hotel man frowned again and Stephanie could have sworn aloud at her obvious faux pas. Any hope that he'd missed it was erased by his next statement.

"You've been here for a bit, then."

It definitely wasn't a question, and his accusing glare dared her to deny it. She chewed on the edge of her lip, knowing she must look guilty as sin. "Just a while," she said finally. "Actually I was trying to cool off and see if I could—"

He cut into her ramblings. "Nevil would have been interested to know you were so close. He had a different idea as to your whereabouts."

"I can't imagine why he'd care."

His thin lips twisted in an unpleasant way. "If you've been here as long as I'm inclined to think, you'd understand that we both have a vested interest. Right now, I want to know where you've left Cole Warner."

Stephanie made a production of dusting the gravel from the seat of her pants. "I'd like to know myself," she said in an uncaring tone. "It looks as if I'll have to pay for my own dinner tonight." She paused long enough to glance at her watch. "If I don't get going, I'll miss my reservation. Nice seeing you again, Mr. Stacy."

"Not so fast." He moved even as she took her first step on the downward trail, and suddenly there was a snub-nosed revolver leveled at her. "I don't think we've covered all the important topics, Miss Church."

Stephanie's eyes widened, amazed at how quickly he'd whipped the gun from the back of his trouser waistband. Her reasoning process wasn't working nearly as fast, she knew. While she was still wondering about making a dash for it on a gimpy foot, he'd grabbed her elbow and shoved her upward toward the summit of the ridge.

"Nevil will have to decide about this," he muttered, clearly annoyed by the newest development. "I knew that we were going to have trouble on this shipment—I could feel it in my bones. If I'd had any sense, I'd have seen you on a plane back to the States instead of letting you hang around poking your nose into somebody else's business."

"I don't know what you're talking about," Stephanie countered, trying to decide which hurt most—her swollen ankle or his iron grip on her arm. "All I know is that this is going to make me late for dinner and I don't have any desire to see your friend Nevil again."

"Believe me," Stacy said in her ear, "the feeling is mutual. Nevil's been doing his damnedest to get you and your friend out of the picture."

She pulled to a stop a few feet from the summit, her shoes scooping up the loose gravel in the process. "You mean he was the one who shoved me into the palm tree on Peter Island?

But he was already on the ferry back to Tortola. I saw him getting off another one the next morning."

"So maybe I was wrong. You can always ask him," he said sarcastically. Stacy seemed to derive satisfaction from her gasp of pain as he twisted her arm again because he added, "That's just a preview of what will happen if you don't cooperate. Now, move."

His final shove almost sent her sprawling, but she managed to struggle up to the summit with Stacy close on her heels.

Although the last rays of daylight were fading fast, it was easy to see why visitors made the effort to view Honeymoon Cove down below. It was a beautiful, peaceful harbor with a crescent-shaped beach of fine white sand. There was also a hint of danger, with rocky cliffs looming at the far end of the cove and bordering the trail as it wound down in a series of switchbacks. The stark outlines of succulents that had survived in the poor soil added another hazard if anyone ventured off the path.

It was Stacy's sharp indrawn breath that jerked her thoughts from the island scenery. Following his gaze, she saw two big power cruisers appear around the end of the island on an apparent collision course with the pair of fifty-foot sailboats that were already bobbing at anchor some one hundred feet from shore.

There was a rubber dinghy with one man in it nearing the bow of one of the schooners.

Since the power cruisers were approaching from the other side, the man obviously hadn't seen them coming.

A steady stream of muttered profanity showed what Stacy thought about it. "The fool," he said, turning back to Stephanie and giving her arm a vicious twist to emphasize his feeling. "Did you know about this, too? Was that why you were lurking around—to be in at the kill?"

"I don't know what you're talking about," she managed, blinking rapidly so he wouldn't see the tears of pain he'd caused. "Is that Nevil in the dinghy?"

"What do you think?" He gave the scene in front of them a disgusted look and then whirled her around to start her down the path toward the other side. "One thing for damned sure, I'm not hanging around here until he starts spilling his guts. By then, I can duck into a nice little anchorage until the heat lets up. The only person who could spoil my game now is you. You'd slow me down if I took you along—and right now you're the only witness against me. At least, the only one who'd count. They'd say Nevil was just trying to save his skin." The man let that sink in as his gaze went impersonally over her. From his opaque expression, he could just as well have been surveying something pulled in on a gaff hook. Something dead on gaff hook, she thought dazedly as he retrieved the automatic from his waistband again and hefted it purposefully in his hand. "To coin a cliché: you were in the wrong place at the wrong time, Miss Church."

Stephanie stared at the gun in horror, vaguely aware how incongruous it sounded that he was still addressing her so formally. But then, Amy Vanderbilt didn't have a chapter to cover "Informal Homicide." It was sheer instinct for preservation that made her argue when he leveled the gun. "Don't be a fool," she said, amazed that she could even talk, under the circumstances. "If you add murder to the list, you'll be in jail for the rest of your life. So far, I imagine all they've got on any of you is a little smuggling. And you can't run far enough to get away," she continued frantically. "You should know that."

Even as she spoke so desperately, she knew she hadn't convinced him. The hardening expression on his face proved it. Ridiculous to imagine that she could. And what a spot to die, she thought hysterically, on a rocky hilltop with crabs crawling all over the place.

Stephanie was so terrified by then that the sudden sound of gunfire from Honeymoon Cove didn't really register. It made Stacy whirl around, however, and start back toward the summit. Before he had gone more than a yard or two, there was a sound of running footsteps on the path below.

Stacy hesitated then, and that made Stephanie realize that she'd never have a better chance to escape.

She lunged past him, giving him a desperate

shove in the process, which caught him unawares. He fell back, struggling to keep his balance and aim the revolver at the same time.

Stephanie cast a desperate glance over her shoulder, only to see him suddenly collapse onto the gravel and stay there.

At the same moment, another heavy hand caught her on the shoulder and spun her around. She screamed—a scream that must have been heard all the way to the end of Virgin Gorda. And then, when she saw it was Cole clutching her, her second scream gurgled into nothingness.

"God in heaven," he gritted out. "I should have known you'd be up to your neck in trouble." Then, looking beyond her at the fallen figure, he added, "So this is where Stacy got to."

When he walked toward him, Stephanie trailed along saying, "Be careful. He's got a gun."

Cole bent over him cautiously to remove it and place it on a nearby rock. "He's also got a lump on his head. What did you do to him?"

"I didn't do anything." A sudden weariness was flooding her whole being as she spoke. "He was going to shoot me to protect his alibi, but then he heard gunfire from the cove. I tried to make a break for it and gave him a shove, but it wasn't that hard."

Cole was still crouched over the inert figure. "You had some unexpected help. He must have stepped on a crab and then had the bad luck to hit his head on this rock. The rock's still in good shape, but the crab didn't make it." He stood up and started to pull the belt from his trousers. "I'd better truss up Mr. Stacy before he comes 'round. Have you got anything to tie his feet?"

Stephanie heard his question and remembered shaking her head. She also remembered thinking that it would be better to hold any future discussions sitting on the ground. It would be a good thing to look out for crabs first, she told herself. She was so busy doing it that she barely heard Cole say forcefully, "Hey, you're not going to faint. For God's sake, Steph, not now. Not now."

It was the last thing she heard for quite a while.

Chapter 9

When she surfaced again—at least to be aware in a hazy way of what was going on—there were two men in uniform carrying her down the trail. Once she roused, they seemed happy to let her walk, but were scrupulous about trying to keep her weight off her swollen foot. Mr. Warner, they said, would see her again at the resort office as soon as he contacted Mr. MacLean aboard the cruiser in the cove.

When she asked about Stacy's condition, they mumbled something to the effect, "He'd be taken care of."

Darkness had fallen by the time they reached the bottom of the trail. She looked around, giving silent thanks that she had two strong policemen beside her with a powerful flashlight to guide their way.

Once they arrived at the resort, she was deposited politely in the deserted office. By then, she was able to assure them that she was perfectly all right aside from a slightly twisted ankle. The policemen looked relieved and then departed to report to their superiors, after telling her that MacLean would probably get her statement later on.

When they were going out the door, a waiter came in bearing a loaded tray of food, which he deposited on the desk in front of her. The smell of coffee was heavenly, and Stephanie found it was no trouble to consume all of the thick turkey sandwich that accompanied it. As she pursued the last bite and surveyed the empty plate, she recalled that females were supposed to exhibit sensibility at a time like this and lose their appetites. Instead, she was peering beneath the edge of her saucer to see if perhaps an after-dinner mint had been added for dessert.

By the time the door opened again, she was considering the bowl of sugar cubes as a desperate measure. Her hand dropped quickly in her lap as she saw the familiar figure of the resort manager she'd met when she checked in.

"Feeling better, are you?" he asked, giving her an anxious look. "We weren't sure if you'd feel like eating, and my wife thought a bowl of consommé would be more appetizing, considering everything." He cast a quick look at the empty tray and a relieved smile came over his face. "I'm glad to see that I was right."

"Everything tasted wonderful, thanks," Stephanie told him truthfully, even as she decided that she could stop by the gift shop on the way back to her cottage and buy a candy bar to fill in her still-empty spaces.

"Is there anything else we can furnish you?"

"Not a thing," she told the man cheerfully. "I'll just go back to my room and clean up. I think I must still have part of your beach sand in my shoes. What's the matter?" The last came when she saw a frown suddenly crease his forehead.

He made an agitated gesture. "About going back to your room, Miss Church. I'm afraid you don't have one. Mr. Warner advised us earlier by radiotelephone that you wouldn't be needing it any longer. I had one of the maids pack your things and they've already been put aboard the *Bagatelle*."

"The *Bagatelle*?" She shook her head slightly as if to clear it. "But where is it?"

"Out in our moorage area," he said, gesturing. "I hope this was all right. I would offer you another room, but your cancellation was snapped up about ten minutes after the hut became available."

Stephanie was still so befuddled by this newest development that she could only nod and stare into space, wondering if Cole had decided to take her to Tortola at the earliest possible moment when his work with Ian and the other authorities was finished.

"Normally we would have waited to check with you, but since Mr. Warner had made your reservation originally, I didn't doubt that it would meet with your approval . . ." The resort manager's voice trailed off and he looked at her hopefully.

"Don't worry about it." She summoned a weak smile in response. "There is one thing you could do for me, though."

"Of course." He gave her a brisk nod, obviously relieved that she wasn't going to raise any difficulties. "Whatever you want—except for a roof over your head."

She nodded, acknowledging his weak attempt at humor. "I need a lift out to the *Bagatelle*, if you could manage it. It would be nice to get aboard and relax."

The worried look came back to his face. "I can certainly understand that, but I think Mr. Warner planned to meet you here."

"Then he'll just have to change his plans." Stephanie's tone didn't leave any leeway for argument. "Perhaps you'd be kind enough to tell him I'm aboard the schooner."

"Whatever you say." The manager gestured expansively as if to say that no wish of hers would be turned down now that the vital decisions had been made. "I'll get Lucas to take you out in one of our boats right away. If you'll just wait here, please."

He hustled away and Stephanie was left wondering if she should settle the bill for her sandwich. Then she pushed the tray farther back on the desktop and stood up. Cole had managed everything so far; he might as well pick up her dinner check. Once they reached Tortola, she'd insist on settling her accounts.

A pleasant-looking young native poked his head around the door at that moment to announce that he was Lucas, and ready to take her out to the *Bagatelle*.

The ferrying operation was carried out without a hitch. The resort launch was considerably bigger than the dinghy from the *Bagatelle*, which she saw secured to the other side of the resort dock. If she'd been a better sailor, she could have taken that back to the schooner by herself, she thought. Then the darkness of the harbor, with just the riding lights of the moored vessels and the strong current swirling around the dock, made her realize that it was a dangerous fantasy.

Apparently Lucas and the manager hadn't even given it a consideration, and she was helped into the resort launch with all the aplomb of visiting royalty.

When Lucas swung the craft alongside the schooner a few minutes later, he made sure that she had successfully negotiated the boarding ladder and was on deck before he gave a cheerful wave of farewell.

The *Bagatelle*'s deck had considerable motion, which wasn't unusual, considering the forceful currents in the anchorage. At first it seemed strange to be back aboard, but by the time she'd reached the stairs leading down into the cabin, she smiled and her hand stroked the railing with real pleasure.

She turned on the overhead light of the cabin and then started to laugh as she surveyed the scene in front of her. Whatever else Cole had been doing during the day, he hadn't wasted any time with housekeeping duties. The bed in the middle of the room still had a blanket tossed at the bottom, and the upper sheet was shoved alongside. The pillows were still at the top of the bed close together and Stephanie's cheeks warmed as she stared at them.

Almost automatically she filled the tea kettle and set it on the stove to boil while she went over to straighten the bed. Her first impulse was to shove the cushions back in place along the wall, and then it looked so comfortable that she decided against it. If she was destined for a long wait before Cole returned, it was certainly more inviting than the cramped quarters of her stern cabin.

By the time the water boiled, the pillows were neatly fluffed and the covers folded at the foot. She went over to make a mug of instant coffee to try and keep awake, unearthing a package of crackers to go with it.

Her eyelids were still drooping after the snack, and she walked over to the stairs and stuck her head above deck to see if the fresh breeze would make her stay awake.

It didn't help any more than the caffeine, and

she could only think that her reaction from that confrontation with Stacy on the ridge was now setting in with a vengeance. Her ankle was throbbing as well, and she stared vexedly down at it. It didn't take a mirror to make her realize that she was going to be black and blue literally from head to toe. "Damn and blast," she muttered, limping over to the edge of the bed.

It wouldn't hurt to rest awhile, she decided, and leaned back against the pillows. She'd hear Cole when he finally returned with the dinghy, and she'd be in better shape to demand an explanation after a short nap.

Sheer exhaustion sent her to sleep almost immediately, but it seemed to Stephanie that she must have endured a series of nightmares instead of a restful doze.

The scene on the hillside replayed in her mind with additional bits of horror that had her moving restlessly on the pillow. When Stacy was pointing the gun at her, a noise sounded in her ear at the instant his finger squeezed the trigger. She shot upright in bed with an almighty shriek and then gasped as she saw Cole stretched out beside her with a resigned look on his face.

"What are you doing here?" she managed to ask.

"I was trying to sleep," he said before relenting as he saw how pale her face was in the dim light of the cabin. "I didn't wake you because I thought you needed some rest."

She nodded and ran her fingers through her tousled hair. "How long have you been here?"

He consulted his watch and swung his legs over the side of the mattress to turn on another lamp at the side of the cabin. "About twenty minutes."

Evidently he'd shed his shirt when he came aboard but had changed into cotton slacks, Stephanie noted as he went over to put some water in the kettle and lit the stove burner beneath it.

"If that's for coffee, aren't you afraid it'll keep you awake?" she asked.

It was a ridiculous comment and Cole's weary reply confirmed it. "My God, after everything that has happened today, it would take more than caffeine to keep me awake tonight. Although, considering the way you were acting a few minutes ago, I believe you'd do better with brandy rather than coffee."

"I hate brandy," she said pettishly, thinking she really must have staged a floor show while she had her eyes closed.

"It's either that or Scotch." He was looking in the cabinet beside the sink as he spoke.

"I hate—"

"Scotch," he finished resignedly. "Okay. How about a sleeping pill? I still have some of those the doctor prescribed for you at Peter Island."

Stephanie got off the mattress as gracefully as possible, since she was still wearing rumpled clothes and a layer of Mosquito Island dirt. "If you think I'm going to take any sleeping pills before you've explained what the deuce has been going on for the last twelve hours, you're the one who needs medicine."

He shrugged and grinned. "Okay. I didn't think you'd want to postpone the explanations, although it seems to me that you could do with a little 'R and R.' "

"I've had some rest, and the notion of relaxing without knowing what happened to Stacy and Nevil is ridiculous," she told him tartly.

He held up his hands in mock surrender. "Okay, okay. At least go wash your face and put on something cooler while I provide a little nourishment."

"I'd settle for tea and crackers," she said automatically, and then, before he could reply, she added, "Remind me to take you out for a decent dinner when we reach Tortola. This diet of toast and coffee or tea and crackers may be good for my waistline, but I think I'm starving to death."

He gave her a gentle shove in the direction of the bathroom. "Stop complaining. Don't forget we had peanut-butter sandwiches for lunch one day."

She lingered at the door of her tiny lavatory. "It's just a good thing we're not spending much more time aboard, or I'd probably get a case of scurvy. Maybe I could sue you—" She broke off as he threatened her with the empty mug. Then she gracefully thumbed her nose at him and closed the door behind her.

When she came out some ten minutes later, she was considerably cleaner and her hair had been brushed until it shone. She'd debated over using makeup, since it was obviously bedtime, but had gone ahead anyhow and used a soft coral lipstick sparingly. Just the barest touch of blusher removed her from the "patient" category and established her back in the land of the living. It was important to change her image in Cole's mind, and if it took a smidgen of artificial color, so be it. Stephanie didn't dwell on the reason why; she just knew that the finished result in the mirror was a great improvement.

She'd heard Cole going up on deck a few minutes earlier, so she wasn't surprised to find the cabin empty at the moment. He had smoothed the pillows on their makeshift bed and tidied the galley in the interval, she noted approvingly as she lingered before going in her stateroom to change clothes.

What to wear was another decision that required some thought. Nothing glamorous: that would be a dead giveaway. She looked longingly at the satin sleep shirt from Peter Island and then shook her head. There was such a thing as being too obvious, dammit!

She finally settled on a pair of white pajamas piped in navy blue. The fabric was imported pima cotton, completely opaque and generously cut. Her swimsuits were considerably more revealing, Stephanie decided, so Cole wouldn't think she was trying for a midnight seduction scene. After a final flick of her hair and making sure that her nose wasn't shiny, she went back in the main cabin.

Cole was adjusting one of the pillows at the foot of the bed, but he looked up and let his glance run quickly over her, although Stephanie suspected that he didn't miss an inch on the way. "I was beginning to wonder if you'd collapsed from heat stroke in your cabin," he said, continuing to punch the pillow into a more comfortable position before sitting down on the edge of the mattress and leaning against it.

While he was making sure the pillow was satisfactorily arranged, Stephanie was noting that he'd changed into pajamas, too. They were the same pajama trousers she'd remembered from Peter Island, and this time he'd donned the blue silk robe. Probably so she wouldn't get any wrong ideas, she decided.

"What's the matter?"

His question brought her head up. "What do you mean?" she asked, puzzled.

"You look unhappy," he said after another hooded glance.

"I'm surprised you don't add 'washed out' and 'god-awful,' " she said, unable to hide the sudden bitterness she felt.

"That didn't occur to me, but I could add 'in a stinking mood.' " There was a definite undercurrent of amusement in his voice. "Are you sure I can't tempt you with Scotch instead of tea?"

She shook her head and kept her attention on the steaming water she was pouring into a clean mug. "Want to share the tea bag?" When there was no answer, she looked up to find his shoulders shaking with laughter.

"Lord, no," he got out finally. "I'll bet you cut coupons out of the Sunday papers, too."

"Doesn't everybody?" she asked innocently, and grinned back at him.

"Well, I have to admit that my mother does. My father gives her a hard time, too."

Stephanie used the rescue of her tea bag from the hot water as an excuse for not meeting his gaze. "Does it bother her?"

"Not in the least. After forty-odd years, I'm sure she's gotten used to it. Are you planning to discuss my family's quirks for the rest of the night?"

Her head shot up at that. "Certainly not. Besides, you were the one who started it."

"So I did." He stretched out more comfortably on the bed. "Now I'm the one who's finishing it. Do you want to come next to me or do you prefer the view from the head of the bed?"

It wasn't what she preferred, Stephanie thought irritably. It was simply safer not to get too close. "I'll try the head of the bed."

"I thought you might." He pushed the other pillow in her direction as she moved to the edge of the mattress.

Before arranging it, she put the mug of steaming tea on the floor within reach and then propped herself on the bed to face him. She observed the belt of his robe had loosened, displaying an inordinate amount of tanned chest. The expanse of smooth skin seemed to draw her gaze like a magnet, and it was an effort to concentrate on retrieving her tea mug.

The silence lengthened between them and finally sheer curiosity brought her gaze up. His eyes narrowed thoughtfully as he surveyed her, but his expression was as unrevealing as ever. When warmth crept under her cheekbones, a flicker of a smile showed at the corner of his mouth.

"So carefully, carefully discreet," he taunted. And then, as she started to move off the bed, he held up a restraining hand. "Okay, relax. I apologize. It's just that you rise so beautifully to the bait each time."

She leaned back in her original position. "Perhaps we could discuss my eccentricities another time. Right now, I'd like to know what you've been doing all day and why I had to be dumped here on Mosquito Island."

He sat up and shoved his pillow into a wedge shape. "My God, this thing is hot!" Then, before she could complain about his changing the subject, he said flatly, "I 'dumped' you, as you so elegantly put it, to keep you away from harm. Which turned out to be ridiculous. If the women's auxilary to the French Foreign Legion is looking for a few good recruits, I'll be glad to supply you with a reference. What in hell were you doing on that ridge with Stacy?"

"Well, you see, I've had this hankering for him all along, and when I had a chance to be alone with . . . Cut it out! I almost spilled the tea." The protest came after she dodged a decorative bunk pillow stored on top of the bedding.

"It's a good thing you didn't. There's not much room on the mattress as it is, and I can't think you'd enjoy eight hours on a wet sheet."

She pursed her lips thoughtfully. "That depends. Right now a cold wet sheet sounds pretty good, but not a hot one. This cabin is like the inside of a laundry."

"That's what happens in this part of the world when you arrive out of season."

Her lips twitched. "And you're changing the subject again."

"So I am." He yawned mightily. "I could think of far more interesting things to do."

"Like sleeping?"

He took a few seconds to consider it. "Sleeping isn't at the top of my list, but it's not far down."

"In that case, maybe you should get on with your story."

"Umm." He settled back against the pillow again. "Okay, after leaving you on the pier this morning, I sailed back to Biras Creek at the far end of the sound. Ian and his people had taken over a place there and it seemed better to report in person. That way, I could tell him what happened last night after I left him."

"You left him?"

Her emphasis on the last word made him frown. "That's right. Earlier in the evening—

when I went ashore. Who did you think I was with?" His inquiring glance focused on her features, apparently aware of her heightened color and reluctance to answer.

Stephanie was darned if she'd admit her suspicions. While she was delighted to learn that he hadn't been cavorting around the resort with an old flame, it was prudent to change the subject as quickly as possible. "I had no idea," she said when she saw that he wasn't going to let her off without an answer. "I didn't really dwell on it. What did Ian have to report when you got in touch with him?"

"That everything was set for the showdown just before dark tonight. He didn't want the patrol boats to appear early and possibly disrupt Nevil's time schedule for the rendezvous. I was to stay out of sight with the *Bagatelle* until the last minute and then I could rejoin you." A rueful grin creased his tanned face for just an instant. "You weren't the only one 'dumped' on Mosquito Island, my love. The men in uniform didn't want a civilian muddling up their plans either, especially since it was obvious that Nevil didn't fall for our cover."

"At least Stacy hadn't completely made up his mind about it." Stephanie was trying to remember his exact words up on the ridge. Then another thought struck her. "But if you had been dismissed from the hunt, what were you doing on the hillside?"

He let out a weary sigh. "Looking for you, of

course. I returned to the island thinking we'd have a relaxing drink and wait around in comfort until Ian came to report on the success of their operation. So I anchored out here and strolled into the resort and found your cottage empty. Then one of the maids reported that she'd seen you heading up the path, and a bellman said that you'd been inquiring about the view of Honeymoon Cove earlier. It was a good thing, because that note you left just said you'd be back soon." He shook his head, remembering. "Even then, I didn't think you were in any danger unless you'd gone all the way to the cove, but I couldn't take a chance. I never dreamed you'd have a confrontation with Stacy. Thank the Lord, Ian had arranged a backup contingent of men on this side of the island just in case Nevil wasn't aboard his schooner."

"He wasn't, was he?"

"Well, his dinghy was so close that he didn't have a hope of escape. None of the crews did. All it required was a boarding party to confirm that the transfer had been in progress and take charge of the evidence."

"How did you hear about all this?"

"After we sent you down the hill, I stayed around to make sure that Stacy didn't get away. I haven't tied anybody up since I worked on knots for a scout merit badge."

"I didn't know you practiced on people for a merit badge."

"Evidently you did it one way—I did it another. Whatever works. Now, where was I?"

"Making sure your knots held on that misera-ble creature." She shuddered as she remembered the expression on the hotel manager's face when he'd confronted her. "He said he was sorry that he had to shoot me, but it still wasn't going to change his mind."

"Rest assured that he sincerely regrets his behavior." Cole didn't raise his voice, but there was an undertone that made Stephanie glad she hadn't stayed around on the ridge to see what happened later.

She strove for a lighter touch. "All I know is that I'm never going to order a crab salad or Newburg again. I'm sorry that Stacy crunched the one that saved me."

"There are quite a few left up there."

"Well, they have my eternal gratitude," she told him truthfully.

"I'm not sorry myself." He crossed his arms over his chest. "Of course, none of this need have happened if you'd stayed in your cottage. What in the devil were you doing up on the ridge in the first place? Had you seen Stacy earlier?"

She made a helpless gesture. "I didn't know it was Stacy. He was too far away when he beached his dinghy, but his behavior seemed a little strange."

"So you decided to follow him. I knew it." Cole lowered his chin and glared at her.

"Well, what was I supposed to do?"

"Some people pay a lot of money to stay in a

place like this where they can relax, take naps, swim in the surf—"

"I'd already taken a nap. By then, I hoped some physical exercise might be therapeutic, so I didn't have time to think. That was your fault."

He raised his palms prayerfully. "I knew that would be the end result. Heaven protect me from feminine logic."

"If you're planning to start a fight, I'm going to bed," she announced.

"That might be the first sensible thing you've said all night," he told her, swinging his feet to the floor.

"Not so fast. I still want to know what Ian and his men found aboard those boats. And why were there two schooners in the cove?"

Cole looked pointedly at his watch.

"You're trying to change the subject again, but I refuse to let you off this time." Stephanie felt a guilty twinge reminding him. There was no denying the weariness of his features, but she wanted to get the whole episode over so they could go on to other things. Or not go on to other things possibly, she thought. But that would have to be faced, too. A forthcoming "moment of truth" between them was inevitable—like a black cat choosing a white blanket for his bed. She tore her mind away from the tempting prospect of beds in general as she asked again, "Why two? I presume that one was Nevil's."

Cole wet his finger and traced an imaginary star in the air. "Go to the head of the class.

Actually our friend Nevil controls quite a fleet of boats, and he's had them coming in to the Virgins for some months now."

"What's wrong with that?"

"Nothing, except the customs people objected to the cargo. They suspected he wasn't just checking out charter sailors."

"I see." Stephanie's lips pursed as she thought about it. "But why here?" she asked finally.

Cole swung his legs back onto the mattress and leaned against his pillow again in surrender. "Because, mate," he said, parodying Nevil's Down Under accent, "this was a bloody profitable place to do the switch." Then, seeing her perplexed look, he went on in his normal tones. "From what the authorities have gotten out of them so far, there was a regular pipeline of contraband coming from South America into the Virgins. Mainly into British territory first. But since the U.S. mainland was their final destination, they needed to transfer stuff to the American Virgin Islands, so conveniently close. Remember I told you about the literally thousands of boats in this area. There's no way the authorities could check on every schooner going in and out of their regular moorages. Are you with me so far?"

"Practically tromping on your heels," Stephanie said, her eyes alight with interest. "And that's why Stacy was in it, too?"

"I imagine so. He had access to a big charter fleet that helped confuse the issue if the authorities started sniffing around. Most of the charters, of course, were completely innocent. Stacy probably did an excellent job managing the resort operation, so he was the ideal recruit for Nevil. Ian thinks Stacy was just a small link in their chain. Nevil was the one with the authority at this end."

Stephanie digested his words and then shook her head slowly. "That's all very well, but how could Nevil have been around to cause our trouble on Peter Island? We saw him getting off the ferry from Tortola the next morning."

"That threw me, too, until I mentioned it to Ian last night. They were keeping watch on Nevil as well, and it turns out he didn't catch the ferry back to Tortola after we'd anchored. Remember, I didn't hang around the pier to make sure. I guess he wanted to see if we were just another pair of tourists, but then you came along to louse up his surveillance."

Stephanie rubbed the side of her forehead absently. "So he had to take his witness out of the picture."

Cole's expression hardened. "Either temporarily or permanently. I don't think he cared by then because he was suspicious of us already."

Stephanie didn't want to dwell on that. "But how did he manage to catch the ferry from Tortola the next morning?"

"Think back," Cole instructed. "We just saw him at the foot of the gangway mingling with the departing passengers. All he had to do was wait and then go on board for the return trip to Tortola, which was what he'd planned all along."

"Then he was on Peter Island overnight." Her eyes widened as she thought what could have happened. "I'm glad we stayed in the hotel."

"So am I—for more reasons than one. I'm also glad that you saved our bacon when he set us adrift in Gorda Sound last night."

"I was just lucky that time." Her glance held his for a moment and then dropped as the silence lengthened between them. "What was the cargo to be transferred tonight?" she asked finally.

"Money. Probably destined for St. Thomas and then on up to Miami for laundering on the mainland. It would be all neatly handled once they got it ashore in American territory. When I first tumbled onto their operation on my other trip, it was precious stones. That night, Nevil got drunk at the resort and was talking too much."

Stephanie nodded soberly. "The beginning of his downfall."

"Well, it hurried it along. The authorities here had been suspicious for some months, but they couldn't pin it down. Probably because they suspected a drug operation, using work boats or small freighters. Stacy admitted tonight that they stuck to small craft—just lots of them. Probably that's why they were successful this long."

"Then Stacy is going to talk?"

"Oh, yes. Don't forget—they've got him on attempted murder as well."

"I hadn't forgotten." A bleak look came over

her face for a moment before her lips curved in an irrepressible grin. "You see, I did come in handy, after all. Even if it wasn't the role you'd selected for me."

Cole took a deep breath and rubbed his forehead. "God, if I'd had any idea . . ."

"Don't be silly," she said severely. "It's been a terrific vacation. Just think, if you hadn't rescued me, I would have been sentenced to a daily ferry trip to St. Thomas and emptying my bank account at the shops over there."

"Instead, I almost got you killed twice and shipwrecked, to boot."

Stephanie could have kicked herself for letting the conversation take such a dismal turn. Apparently the only way to get him out of the doldrums was to sacrifice some of her feminine pride. "If you must know," she admitted finally, "the only time that I was really unhappy was when you put me ashore this morning and sailed off into the sunrise. I thought I'd never see you again."

It took an instant for her to gather her nerve and meet his glance after that. The color had run up his cheekbones and his gray eyes were fixed on her face. As she watched, she saw him let out an obvious breath of relief and sit up straight on the edge of the bed. "That does make it easier," he said in rough tones that she'd never heard before. "Maybe you'd come a little closer." He was reaching over to pull her across his lap as he spoke. "We have to plan the rest of our cruise."

By then, Stephanie's heart had abandoned its regular cadence and was thumping violently. She was sure Cole could feel it as his hand fumbled momentarily with the buttons of her pajama coat before moving gently but possessively over her, leaving her skin on fire with longing. And then his mouth came down, eventually finding her lips in a kiss that made time stand still.

When he finally raised his head, he shook it slightly and gave her glowing face a wry look. "If you knew how long I've been wanting to do that."

Stephanie settled happily against his shoulder, aware that they were merely postponing the time before desire would flare again. "You certainly hid it well. I thought you felt like tossing me overboard whenever I came close."

His crooked grin took years from his face and made her wonder why she'd ever thought him stern. "You were only on board about fifteen minutes before I realized that you were the kind of woman I'd been waiting for all my life," he confessed. "But I sure as hell didn't plan to involve you in any danger. Then you got hurt—"

"So you had to look after me. That's when I started falling in love," she confessed. "Anybody who could be so kind to a comparative stranger . . ." She broke off as he leaned over and kissed her again, softer this time but just as nice.

"Some stranger," he murmured finally. "Even

with a black eye, you were exactly what I wanted. I haven't changed my mind. That's why I think we should sail to St. Thomas tomorrow. Once we're back under the flag, we can find the quickest way to get married." He felt her sudden indrawn breath and gave her an anxious look. "That's all right with you, isn't it? After all, three days together in a sailboat translates to at least six months' courtship on shore. But if you'd rather do it by the book . . ." This time he broke off as she slid her hands lovingly around his shoulders and pulled him down to her waiting lips.

When they broke apart that time, they were both breathing hard. She put a soft finger up to trace his jaw as she managed to say, "Enough talking. You need to get some rest. We have a long sail ahead of us tomorrow."

"I suppose you're right." Cole sat up, but his hand stopped her when she started to do up the buttons on her pajama coat. "I like it that way," he said simply, and then looked around. "You can't sleep back in that cabin of yours. There isn't any ventilation."

Stephanie pretended to consider it before nodding. "Yours isn't much better. When we buy our own boat, we'll have to check out the sleeping facilities more carefully."

"Right. That only leaves this bunk. We shared it last night without any problems. So, if it doesn't bother you . . ." He looked at her hopefully.

"Not a bit," she said without hesitation. "I think we'll do fine. After all, we are two adults."

"Engaged to be married."

She nodded. "That certainly makes it respectable." She leaned over to fix their pillows together and then looked at him, as if just remembering. "Besides, we still have that loaf of bread to preserve the conventions."

"No, we don't." His tone was calm but firm. "I tossed it overboard a little while ago when you were getting undressed. I'd been planning to do it all day."

The sudden smile she gave him seemed to light up the entire cabin. "Thank heavens! If you hadn't, my love, I certainly would have," she confessed, and surrendered happily back in his fierce embrace.

27 million Americans can't read a bedtime story to a child.

It's because 27 million adults in this country simply can't read.

Functional illiteracy has reached one out of five Americans. It robs them of even the simplest of human pleasures, like reading a fairy tale to a child.

You can change all this by joining the fight against illiteracy.

Call the Coalition for Literacy at toll-free **1-800-228-8813** and volunteer.

Volunteer Against Illiteracy.
The only degree you need is a degree of caring.